HER WICKED HIGHLANDER

Glennoe Highlanders #2

NICOLA DAVIDSON

HER WICKED HIGHLANDER © Nicola Davidson
First Edition: May 2022
ISBN: 9780473729721 (Paperback)
Country of Production: New Zealand
Cover: Dar Albert at Wicked Smart Designs
Editor: Sabrina Darby

CHAPTER 1

Glennoe Castle, on the shores of Loch Etive
Western Highlands
March 1505

Many would find it exceedingly odd, a woman of forty-two summers kneeling naked in supplication at her bedchamber window. For Lady Maude MacIntyre, it was a daily ritual.

A full year ago, death had finally dragged away the cruelest husband in Scotland. But while she continued having the visions that lit such a clear path for others, her own future remained stubbornly hidden and her most fervent prayer unanswered.

Clasping her hands, Maude arched her back so the rising sun bathed her skin in enchanted light. Then she lifted her beseeching gaze upward.

"For twenty-six years, I did everything asked of me. Wed a laird I neither loved nor desired to conceive my Callum. Fostered Alastair, and raised both into fine men. Sent them to the royal tourney in Stirling to win dear Isla and the love of the clan..."

Her head dipped, tears trickling down her cheeks.

"Mistake me not, I have much to be grateful for. My boys found bliss in a trio and I'll be a grandmother in autumn. I heal others mostly without impediment and the MacIntyre clan now enjoys peaceful prosperity. But I beg thee...after a life of marital misery, may I not discover love for myself? To know pleasure and comfort in the arms of my chosen man?"

As usual, the heavens remained resolutely silent.

In despair, Maude snatched up her brocade robe and dressed. Thankfully no one was here to witness such weakness; bad enough to be English in the Highlands, let alone possess white-blond hair, unnatural violet eyes, and visions that had first occurred in her sixteenth summer. If she'd been anyone other than the laird's wife, and now the laird's mother, certain villagers would've long ago drowned her in the loch.

A harsh knock on the bedchamber door jolted her from such bleak thoughts, and Maude slowly stood. After crossing the room, she opened her door to the startling sight of a stone-faced MacIntyre guard with a hissing, clawing child dangling from his meaty fist.

Saints alive. Sorcha Wright.

The poor mite appeared much younger than her eight summers; red hair a tatted mess, tunic threadbare, and face smudged with dirt. But since her father and mother had been killed in a raid back in August, Sorcha insisted on staying in their mountain dwelling next door to her uncle.

The child didn't roam. Why would she be out at this hour?

Maude's neck prickled. "Yes?"

"Lady," said the guard with a curt nod. "I found the bairn wandering in the clearing, so brought her to the castle kitchens. But she ran straight to your herb garden to *steal*."

"Did not," spat Sorcha, as she attempted to bite the guard. "Just needed some lavender. To help."

"Help who?" asked Maude, her heart now thudding frantically.

Sorcha's blue gaze was equally fierce and terrified. "Uncle Keir. He's injured verra bad."

Maude gasped.

No. Please no.

Keir Wright was the enormous, ebony-haired Highlander she'd been forbidden to tend or even speak to, due to her powerful attraction to him. Every battle scar Keir gained, every illness he'd endured had been agonizing, knowing he suffered without treatment solely because of her husband Donald's spiteful jealousy. Then, two years ago, Keir had broken Donald's nose in a brawl, been dismissed from his post as captain of the guards, and banished to live on the cold and rugged slopes of Ben Cruachan. That had been the worst blow, being unable to see him each day. But even after Donald's passing, Keir had stayed away and she didn't know why.

Now he was badly injured. What if he died?

No. Not while there was breath in her body. For this time she *could* go to him. Tend him as she'd always longed to do. Perhaps even find out the truth.

"Leave Sorcha with me," said Maude abruptly.

The guard's lip curled. But he nodded, dropped his burden with an unforgiving thump, and left the room.

Crouching down, Maude tried to smile reassuringly at Sorcha. "Can you tell me what happened?"

The child scowled. "I'm no thief."

"I know. But if you tell me what you saw or heard, I can decide what's to be done."

"Uncle Keir always puts out food for me. But not last night. So today I opened the shutter and jumped through a window in his dwelling. He lay on the floor, all shivering and sweaty. When he was out hunting, his foot slipped on gravel and he slid down a ridge. A big rock cut his leg and it's bleeding lots. He said to fetch the blacksmith because ye won't tend him. So I thought if I just got some lavender..."

Maude winced, the words a dagger to her heart. But how could she explain cruel husbands to a little girl? "I'll help him."

Hope dawned in Sorcha's eyes. "Truly?"

"Yes. I'll pack my herbal satchels then inform the laird that I'll miss morning chapel and be away for a while. You shall go to the kitchens to wash your face, and eat your fill of buttered bread and small ale."

"Don't take charity," said Sorcha, raising her small chin.

"That wasn't a request," replied Maude, hardening her voice. "Go."

The child turned and sprinted away.

Her stomach churning relentlessly, Maude halted and pressed a fist to her lips. But she couldn't shatter now, not when there was still a chance to save Keir. She needed to behave like a vastly experienced, steady-handed healer, not someone terrified of losing their lover.

He's not your lover. You've never even kissed, despite all those prayers for it.

The thought hit like a bucket of frigid loch water, and rather remarkably, cleared her head. Swiftly, Maude discarded her robe to dress in her special healer's tunic, a dark brown ankle-length garment made of heavy linen and secured at her waist with a girdle, and a warm cloak. When tending patients, she opted for comfort and ease of movement, so never wore a petticoat or hood, and certainly not a gown of costly fabric with a train. Then she stuffed her sturdy leather satchel with a second tunic, fresh shift, and woolen stockings, for it remained icy cold on the mountain in early spring.

Next, she hurried into the adjoining chamber that served as her apothecary to fetch supplies. The pungent scents of peppermint and ginger were soothing, although the clutter of parchment and quills, leather-bound Latin medical texts, ancient recipes, countless jars, pestles and mortars, and half-open drawers of cut, dried herbs no doubt alarmed others who didn't understand her methods.

But what to take?

Maude added several jars to her satchel: coneflower salve to treat wounds, lavender to heal and relax, peppermint to cool. Also bog moss to halt bleeding, yarrow for fever, and white willow bark if his pain was unbearable.

"Lady Mother. We hear you go to Ben Cruachan?"

Maude dropped an assortment of fresh linen bandages into the satchel side pocket, then glanced up to smile briefly at her beloved family who all stood in the chamber doorway. Fair-haired, scholarly Callum, the laird of Clan MacIntyre. His ebony-haired, swordfighter wife Isla, who never wore gowns, only shirt and hose. And their lover Alastair, like hewn rock behind them, brown-haired and brawny. "My sons. Daughter. Yes. I am urgently needed for a serious injury."

Alastair folded his arms. "Keir Wright?"

"Indeed," she replied, more sharply than intended. "And none of you may even consider forbidding it. Keir is not ill-tempered, even though he broke a nose."

Callum made a frustrated sound, an hourly act for a Scottish laird. "I'm aware. That is why I had Gavin invite him to return to the village. *Twice*. But Keir refused."

Maude grimaced. As Gavin MacTier had replaced Keir as captain of the guards, she wasn't entirely sure the message had been delivered with the goodwill intended. Yet Keir remained on the mountain. "He did refuse."

"Imagine that, a Highland man stubborn as an ornery

bull," Isla said pertly as she cradled the slight swell of her belly. "They're usually so reasonable and obliging."

"A truth," said Maude, unable to halt a snort.

"Here, now," chided Alastair, as both he and Callum sent Isla looks that made her cheeks pinken.

Oh.

Maude sighed. In the past she might have sworn Keir gazed at her like that—gruff tenderness and fierce lust together. But obviously she'd been mistaken, for he'd never come to claim her.

Callum cleared his throat. "Guards will accompany you, Mother. Oh, and here, a letter arrived from the king."

Brightening, she took the missive and added it to her satchel. Her longtime friend James's twice-monthly letters always entertained with their outrageous bawdiness, court news, and whatever learning he currently held close to his heart. It would be a treat to read once Keir was better. "Thank you. As for guards, they may accompany me to the clearing and no further. You know I don't permit others underfoot when treating a patient. I'll be quite safe and shall return in three or four days. Blessings on you all."

The trio looked unconvinced, but understanding her ways, eventually nodded. Maude kissed each on the cheek before hurrying from the herbal chamber.

She only prayed it wasn't too late.

To lose Keir before they'd even had a chance... unthinkable.

He was going to die.

Alas, not felled on a noble battlefield or protecting his home. Not as a cherished elder in a soft bed, surrounded by loved ones and ready for his eternal rest. No, he was going to die alone, perched on a rickety wooden chair in a small, dungeon-like dwelling on the side of a cursed mountain because he was, quite plainly, a fool.

Gritting his teeth against the relentlessly clawing pain, Keir Wright glanced with fever-blurred vision at his lower leg. While the surrounding skin was ominously warm and dark pink, the actual wound was a mess of gouged flesh, oozing blood, embedded dirt and gravel, even a little grass. Far worse: the injury was entirely his own fault. Trying to be clever in his deerstalking, he'd attempted to climb a bank like a mountain goat rather than a man with forty-five summers behind him, slipped on some icy gravel, and slid down several feet of jagged rockface. His left calf had borne the brunt of the fall, and knowing he would perish swiftly in the frigid mountain air if he didn't make it back before sunset, he'd half-lurched, half-crawled home.

That was his second foolish act. A quick death would have been preferable to this slow, agonizing descent into purgatory. Here, when his mind regained moments of clarity, it taunted him with his failures: not finding the remaining few Campbells responsible for killing his younger brother Burke and sister-in-law Fiona during the weaving house raid. Not being a proper uncle to Sorcha, one who could set aside his raging grief to comfort and care for her, even if bairns utterly baffled him. Not knowing the taste of Lady Maude MacIntyre's lips, the bliss of being deep inside her as she screamed her pleasure...never cradling her in his arms as they slept, or his most fervent desire: hearing her murmur words of love.

Aye, he had many failures to confess. Many regrets.

But it was too late for him now. In truth, he'd sent Sorcha to the village for the blacksmith only so she didn't witness his passing; the bairn had endured far too much already. No smithy ritual could save him. His only chance might be a highly skilled and experienced healer like Lady Maude. But she'd always refused to treat him, something he'd never understood. Even the worst of the clan, the mean-spirited wives and falsely pious husbands who called her Witch, knew the miracle of her salves and tonics. They had all felt the brisk, gentle touch of her nimble fingers as she stitched a cut, eased a burn, or guided a babe into the world. How many times as he'd lain in bed with battle wounds or some illness had he whispered her name? Offered his very soul for her help?

But she'd never come. Not to him. When he'd asked Donald why, the laird had shrugged and said Keir's crude ways, lack of learning, and poor service to his betters particularly offended the lady.

A snapping spark in the smoldering fireplace disturbed those dark thoughts; both a blessing and a curse. His leg wound hurt more than any sword or dagger cut, his entire body ached, and he was both weary beyond measure and thirstier than someone adrift at sea. Worse, he was surrounded by bad stenches: the metallic tang of fresh and dried blood, wet muddy wool, and a little piss on his ruined hose because the privy he'd dug outside was a thousand miles away, five steps from the east wall of the dwelling.

"Why can't I just *die?*" he muttered, closing his eyes.

The sound of voices outside almost made him laugh. He'd asked the question and now been answered; those of the Unseelie Court had arrived to drag him down to purgatory. The knock at the door was strange though. He'd always assumed they would just burst in with claws slashing, eyes burning, and unholy oaths spilling from their fanged mouths.

"Uncle Keir?"

Devil take it, the unseelie sounded like Sorcha. Except worried. So very, very worried. Deceitful bastards.

"Away with ye," he tried to snarl, yet even to his own ears his voice was weak and scratchy. "I need no help to perish."

"Hush, Keir. There'll be no death wishes in my presence."

He blinked heavy eyelids. *Deceitful bastards* wasn't nearly strong enough to describe the unseelie. Now they wanted him to believe Lady Maude stood in his dwelling? Aye, but they were cunning and evil. The way they'd spoken just like her, that low husky tone that still held strong echoes of England even after all these years in Glennoe.

"I'll talk how I please in my own damned home," Keir replied irritably, his gesture to send the unseelie back from whence they came almost sending him face-first onto the floor. That would be bad. It had taken hours and much blood loss to heave his massive body up onto the carved wooden chair. He'd wanted to at least make it a little difficult for the wildlife to devour his corpse.

"What you'll do is sit still so I may examine your leg."

Keir frowned. How strange that they would speak so pertly...and even stranger offer to help. He slowly lifted his chin, fully opening his eyes so he might glare at the unseelie face-to-face before they dragged him away.

God's blood.

Shock lanced through him at the sight of Lady Maude standing a few feet away clutching a bulging leather satchel, several bushels of heather strapped to her back. Even dressed in a simple brown tunic, the woman was uncommonly, ethereally beautiful. Long white-blond hair like a crown of moonbeams and eyes the purple of the finest Highland heather. Creamy skin that always carried the fragrance of the herbs she used most, like lemon balm and peppermint. A rounded arse made for a lover's spanking, and ample breasts to fill his palms.

A sound of dismay tore from his throat as his cock stirred. Desiring his laird's wife, a learned, highborn Englishwoman had cost him everything—yet it seemed neither time, punishment, nor her previous indifference could dull his lust.

"I sent for the blacksmith," he growled, as anger and relief and need warred within his pain-fogged mind. "Where is Sorcha?"

His niece appeared from behind the healer, her face surprisingly clean but her chin jutting stubbornly. "I went to the castle garden to borrow some herbs but the guard caught me and took me to Lady Maude. She said I had to wash my face and eat buttered bread and small ale and then she packed her satchels and told the laird she wasn't going to chapel but coming with me for a few days. So there."

He blinked at the detailed explanation, the most words she'd spoken to him since the death of her mother and father. Barely ten feet separated their dwellings, but it may as well have been an entire loch. Sorcha remained there because unlike his rough existence, her dwelling had many comforts, but she did accept the breakfast bread and bowl of stew or broth for supper he left out for her. Sometimes Sorcha sat on the steps wrapped in one of her mother's shawls to watch him train with his sword or prepare meat he'd hunted, but she never ventured closer. Grief had united yet divided them, for how could he ask forgiveness when he'd failed her so badly? When even he didn't know the path forward out of the darkness?

"Well said, my dear," announced Lady Maude, bestowing an approving nod in Sorcha's direction. "Now I'm going to take a closer look at this leg of your uncle's. You were right to fetch help; the wound is serious."

Embarrassed at his weakness, the state of his clothing and the shabbiness of his dwelling that made the lady seem like a diamond in a heap of mud, a part of him still wanted to send her away. But oh, the thought of Maude MacIntyre touching him...

Keir grunted his agreement and was rewarded as she set her satchel and the heather down to lean forward, the pose offering a prime view of plump breasts swelling above the square neckline of her tunic. If that wasn't enough to silence his doubts, she proceeded to press the back of her hand against his forehead, the satiny coolness of her skin against his fevered brow more welcome than a gulp of the finest ale.

"Too hot," he mumbled, nudging her with his head so she might cool the rest of his face. When those enchanted hands gently cupped his cheeks then smoothed back the wild tangle of long, silver-touched black hair so it didn't annoy him further, he groaned in relief. Yet he was so weary his eyes kept closing.

"I know," she replied, her voice oddly uneven. "But I'm here now. All will be well, I swear."

She had arrived here in time thanks to Sorcha's courage— Keir's wound hadn't putrefied and poisoned his blood, a deadly malady not even her extensive abilities could halt. His leg did need careful cleaning and binding though, and he'd certainly be receiving some robust doses of white willow bark tea to manage his pain and fever. But to know she wouldn't lose him to this injury was such a relief she could scarcely speak.

Maude took several deep breaths to gather her wits. She had much to do.

"Sorcha," she said as calmly as possible, while continuing to stroke Keir's face because she couldn't make herself stop, "Can you do me a great favor?"

"Suppose I could."

"To assist your uncle, I need fresh cobwebs. Not spiders, just the webs. And the fattest, stickiest snails you can find. Take that bowl over there to carry them."

Sorcha's gaze narrowed. "For a spell? Are ye a witch, then?"

Not in the way I'm often accused. Just a healer, a soothsayer, who works only in love and light.

"No," said Maude. "But nature provides many gifts to keep the unseelie away and cure the fever and festering that hurts those we care about."

"Oh. Aye, I can find cobwebs and snails. If ye turn witch though…"

The little girl's words trailed off, her gaze threatening such dire retribution that Maude's heart broke for her agonizing losses, the fear she was trying valiantly to conceal. "No dark arts, I swear," she said softly.

Once Sorcha hurried outside, Maude studied Keir closely. His sweat-soaked linen shirt clung to his massive shoulders like a second skin. His flushed cheeks and pallor contrasted starkly with the black beard that covered his jaw and chin, and his hazel eyes were cloudy with pain. First, she needed to stop the bleeding and cool him down. After that she could attend to cleaning and binding the wound.

"Keir," she began briskly. "I'm going to—"

"I like it when ye say my name. I like your voice. Even if ye are *English*."

Maude pressed her lips together, torn between laughing and sobbing. A chivalrous knight who spouted poetry and extravagant compliments Keir was not, and she liked him all the better for it. So many conversations, so many moments that might have made life at Glennoe more bearable, had been stolen by Donald's spite…and that was unforgiveable. "Why thank you."

"How will ye treat my leg?"

"I'll stop the bleeding with bog moss. Then give you a sponge bath to bring down the fever, and white willow bark tea to dull the pain."

"A sponge bath for my fever?" Keir mumbled, his head lolling. "Ha. Just confess ye wish to see me naked."

I do.

"Shhh," she replied, before the distracting thought could lodge in her mind.

After emptying her satchel of supplies, Maude dragged a small wooden footstool over to his chair so she could perch beside him. Working swiftly, she used handfuls of bog moss to soak up the blood trickling from the wound. Then she wet a sponge in tepid water—cold water only compelled a feverish body to remain hot—and bathed his face and neck, all while murmuring an ancient chant of healing and protection.

Keir sighed, the grooves around his eyes and mouth easing. "Mmmm."

She smiled and picked up some silver embroidery shears. They easily cut away his ruined shirt, exposing a hairy chest and arms sculpted with muscle. A swordfighter's arms. Her fingers itched to stroke the crisp hair, to trace each old scar that bore witness to his life as a guard and a hunter, but ruthlessly suppressing the urge, she instead sponged his chest and armpits to cool him down. It was only when she reached the top of his hose that a paw-sized hand abruptly gripped her wrist.

"There's...piss," said Keir, shame clear on his face.

"A good, normal bodily occurrence," she replied firmly. "That tells me your innards are doing what they should and haven't been affected by a humor imbalance."

"Are ye going to bleed me?"

Maude shuddered. She had never adhered to that all-too-common practice. In her experience with battle wounds, losing more blood further weakened bodies rather than corrected an imbalance. Yet another reason she was called witch, but she would always treat each patient on what she saw, smelled, and felt rather than mindlessly following men and their stubborn old ways. "No. You've decorated the floor enough, I believe."

He grunted, his head slumping forward onto her shoulder, before sliding lower onto her breasts. "Then I'll rest for a bit on this soft pillow."

It might have been amusing, but looking around his dwelling, there was no softness in his life. Banishment had been an overly harsh punishment. Why hadn't he left this cold and lonely place when invited to?

Somehow, she balanced his head while bathing his abdomen. Then she carefully slid the sponge under hose to wash his groin. When her fingertips nudged an impossibly large cock, even while flaccid, her cheeks flushed hotly.

Keir frowned, his lips brushing the top of her right breast. "Forgive me. Cannae fuck you today. Maybe tomorrow."

Maude almost gasped at the jolt of sensation that arrowed directly between her legs. She had indeed lost her wits. Neither the kiss nor the words were an invitation; the man was out of his head with pain and fever and didn't know what he was saying. But her pleasure-starved body didn't care; the many times alone in bed when she'd touched herself had not provoked anything like that.

If only he was well and his invitation real...

After resettling Keir upright on the chair, Maude stoked the fire in the hearth and set a pot of well water to boil for the willow bark tea. Then she propped up his leg on the foot-stool, cut away the remnants of his hose, and began the painstaking process of cleaning out the jagged, angry-looking wound with pincers, a small, sharp dagger, and a strong infusion of yarrow. Praise be to Heaven, the cut wasn't as deep as she'd feared.

He grimaced, one hand gripping his thigh as she pressed and pulled to ease out the gravel and dirt, dabbed it with more bog moss when it bled, then thoroughly rinsed the area. "Bit sore."

Most patients would be screaming right now. Or unconscious.

"Is she hurting ye, Uncle?"

They both glanced up to see Sorcha in the doorway holding a full bowl of snails and cobwebs, the scowl on her face so like Keir's that Maude almost smiled.

"Nae," mumbled Keir. "The lady is...er..."

"I'm cleaning his leg," said Maude briskly. "I must get all the bad bits out first. How many snails, Sorcha?"

"Ten."

Keir inclined his head. "Good lassie."

"Wasn't hard," said Sorcha, blushing as she marched forward to set the bowl down beside the footstool. "I'll stay a bit longer. Have to make sure she's not casting spells."

"Of course," said Maude. "Well, now you're back, I can bind this nice clean wound with those sticky cobwebs."

"What do the snails do?" asked Sorcha eventually, after Maude wrapped the white cobwebs around Keir's leg then placed the snails all over the damaged flesh.

"They dance. Their trail helps a wound heal. Eases it from hurting so much."

Keir swayed as he peered down at his calf. "Are they dancing or dueling?"

Sorcha giggled. "*Uncle.* Snails cannae duel. Or dance."

"They can do both. Only in moonlight, though," said Maude. "Now, who is hungry? Not you, Keir, you'll have nothing but willow bark tea. Sorcha, shall we have oatcakes for supper? There is also cheese, sliced venison, and sweetmeats from the castle kitchens. You've earned it, after collecting such fine cobwebs and snails."

"Aye. But then I have to go home. To guard it."

Maude nodded as she unpacked the food satchel and set out plates for them both; ignoring when Sorcha slipped an oatcake and a handful of sweetmeats into her girdle pocket. Then, after gulping down some food, she prepared the willow bark tea with honey to sweeten, and helped Keir sip it down.

When the sun began to set and Sorcha retreated to her own dwelling, Maude opened the mattress covering on Keir's bed and removed the old straw, tossing it into the fireplace to burn. The bushels of heather she'd brought would do much better.

"Dinnae need a fancy bed," said Keir, frowning. "Ye must be tired."

She sniffed and continued to stuff the covering full of dried heather stalks and flowers until it was properly plump. Then she made up the bed with fresh linen. "Too late, you've got one. Now you can try it. Here, I'll help you."

Once Maude removed the snails and set them free, she lightly bandaged the wound, wrapped an arm about his waist, and shuffled him over to the bed to lie down.

"Looks well enough, I suppose," he said, but a soft groan escaped when he sank back into the welcoming embrace of heather mattress, pillows, and cool linen. Soon, Keir was fast asleep.

Maude smoothed his hair and offered another chant, imploring the heavens for peaceful rest and swift healing of his flesh. Then she yawned and pressed a hand to her aching lower back. She *was* tired and the bed looked so very inviting; the mattress large enough that she could easily stretch out and have a short nap without disturbing him. After that she could light candles and tidy the mess, before curling up on a chair in front of the fireplace.

Decision made, she removed her tunic, lay close to the edge of the bed and closed her eyes.

An hour's rest was all she needed.

CHAPTER 2

Despite the fact that his bones ached from sword fighting and his head felt woolly from too much ale, all was right in Keir's world. The birds were chirping a merry dawn chorus, he slept on the most comfortable heather bed in Scotland, and his latest bedmate lay securely nestled against him.

Ah, but he'd chosen well. Slender, yet with ample breasts and arse, just as he liked. She also had a pleasingly fresh scent about her, a blend of lemon and peppermint, almost like Lady Maude MacIntyre. That was another shameful secret he would take to his grave; how often he'd instructed a fair-haired lover to sponge herself with herbed water so she might smell like the laird's wife and he could imagine, just for a moment, that it was Lady Maude on her hands and knees in front of him, moaning and bucking and begging for more.

Wanting to hold onto the dream for just a while longer, Keir nuzzled his bedmate's neck without opening his eyes, allowing his teeth to graze the tender flesh before a flick of his tongue soothed the sting. She whimpered, the needy sound hardening his cock to stone. Aye, the wench certainly required pleasuring. Her perfect rounded arse rubbed rest-lessly against him, and underneath her linen shift where his hand cupped her bare breast, the nipple near-stabbed his palm.

"Easy, sweet," he murmured, lightly pinching the taut peak he would soon be sucking deeply into his mouth. She whimpered again, louder this time. But sounds weren't enough. His bedmates knew he liked to hear them plead for release in the simplest, crudest of terms. If they sought a courtly man who would kiss their hands, read them poetry, and sing odes to their lips, his was not the right bed. Keir Wright was a raw Highlander who was happiest fighting or fucking. "I ken ye hunger for pleasure. But rules are unbreak-able. Ye must beg for what's needed."

Her ragged moan echoed in the bedchamber, yet still she did not speak. Instead, her soft, cool fingers interlaced with his and tentatively pushed his hand from her breast down her stomach, until it rested just on her shift-covered mound. Understanding dawned. His bedmate wished to play a game of virtuous maiden led astray by lusty warrior, an astonish-ingly frequent favorite among wenches. As though he would ever cast stones over their number of lovers.

Keir exhaled slowly and trailed his fingers lower until he felt the hem of her shift. Then he dragged it up, exposing the satiny skin of her inner thighs, the crisp hair of her bush, and the delicate dewy folds concealed beneath. His mouth watered to taste such a bounty, to mark that soft skin with his beard as he plunged his tongue deep. But as he'd told her, rules were unbreakable.

"Something to say?" he asked lazily, nuzzling her neck once more. "Whatever ye want, ye need only ask. Your pearl sucked until it is dark pink and swollen? My fingers rubbing and stroking? Or perhaps you're just a greedy wench wanting that tight virgin cunt stuffed so full of cock you'll still feel me inside a week hence."

Her gasp of outrage made him frown.

What was wrong with that? She had started the game, wearing a modest shift to bed like a nun, and shyly pushing his hand between her legs. Hell, she'd *whimpered*. Like having her neck kissed and nipple pinched were new and wondrous experiences...wait. Was his bedmate vexed because a battle had kept him too long from home and hearth and she'd been neglected? Obviously, he needed to remedy the matter. Several screaming, writhing releases could always be relied upon to sweeten a woman's temper.

Keir stretched and began to roll over, intending to settle between her thighs so he could feast upon his favorite dish: sweet succulent cunt. But white-hot agony speared through his lower leg, robbing him of breath, and remembrance crashed against his skull like a blacksmith's anvil.

This isolated mountain dwelling.

An ungainly fall, festering cut, and burning, disorientating fever.

Lady Maude MacIntyre.

His heavy eyelids wrenched open; confirming the nightmare of his own making.

There she was. The laird's mother, the healer who had finally decided to offer him care and traveled from the castle to save his worthless soul...and this was how he repaid her: behaving like an unscrupulous bastard. He'd spoken lewdly, something she did not like. Worse, he'd laid hands on her. Now the lady, finally free of his foul embrace, had scrambled away to perch on the other side of the heather bed. Her cheeks were rosy red, her steady healer's hands trembling as she attempted to tie the bodice of her shift, those full breasts rising and falling as she gulped in air.

Lady Maude MacIntyre, a woman of honor and position,

the rumored lover and longtime friend of the King of Scotland himself...and he'd treated her like a tavern wench, biting her neck and pinching her nipple and promising to fuck her hard. She hadn't been rubbing against his cock to entice him, she'd been trying to *escape*. Push his hand *away*. Not whimpering or moaning with need, but *distress*. Because he was so far beneath her. Crude and unlearned.

Sick shame filled him and his stomach roiled.

"Lady," he rasped, attempting to sit up without further inflaming his injured leg. Although, right now it was hard to know which hurt more: that or his engorged cock. "Forgive me. I was...out of my head. I would not touch the laird's mother. A skilled healer doing naught but her duty. Not ever. It won't happen again."

She didn't reply or even acknowledge his remorse, instead turning away to snatch up her tunic, yank it on, and smooth the dark brown fabric. After an endless wait, Lady Maude turned back and regarded him, her face calm and composed. "I'll set some water to boil and make you more white willow bark tea."

Keir's gaze narrowed. The lady was *too* calm, *too* composed. However, those stormy violet eyes told a quite different tale. "Your face says nothing happened, but your gaze is a tempest waiting to unleash. Why not free your anger? I deserve it and more."

Lady Maude laughed, but it wasn't a sound of amusement. "As you just reminded me, I am the laird's mother. A healer. Anger would be unbecoming. Now, do you need to use the privy? I will escort you so you do not fall and ruin all my hard work. Or that of Sorcha's snails."

He gritted his teeth at the cool reply, but devil take it, he did need the privy. And the way his leg still throbbed, her help would be required. He was proud and foolish, but not quite enough to reopen a wound only now starting to heal.

"Aye, I do. There is a clean...well, mostly clean shirt hanging on that hook over there. And short hose. If ye dinnae mind fetching them."

"Of course."

While Keir sat on the edge of the bed and slowly, carefully dressed himself in the billowing linen shirt and knee-length hose, Lady Maude bustled about in front of the fireplace with a fresh pot of water and her herb satchel. Then, with her arm impersonally about his waist, they began the endless journey to the outdoor privy at the rear of the dwelling. To think he'd always considered his home small. Ha. It already seemed like they'd walked halfway to Stirling.

She graciously turned her back while he relieved himself, and he was able to kick some dirt into the hole, wash his hands in the small bowl of rainwater, and dry them with a scrap of old linen without assistance. He would certainly need her for the return journey though. While the bracing mountain air had cleared his woolly head, he still felt so damned tired and his leg *ached*. Perhaps another tankard of that willow bark tea wouldn't be the worst thing.

To his surprise, Lady Maude also made use of the privy rather than insisting on a chamber pot, and he in turn looked away to give her privacy. After she'd washed and dried her hands, she escorted him back inside to the heather bed.

"I can sit in the chair," he grumbled, even as sweat gathered at his temples and he gazed longingly at the soft pillows.

"You'll get back into bed and rest," she replied tartly, glaring as she near-shoved him onto the mattress. "That is how a body heals. Not by being a stubborn Highland block-head. There is nothing manly about falling off a chair and kissing the floor."

"Sharp-tongued wench," Keir muttered as he sank once more into the comforting embrace of sweet heather and cool linen. "To think I believed ye kind and gentle."

Lady Maude's cheeks went ruby red. "I'm no saint. Have you not heard the news? I'm a witch! Have a care, lest I snap my fingers and your cock falls off."

His jaw dropped at the spirited and bawdy outburst, and said cock stirred once more.

This was a side of Lady Maude MacIntyre he'd never seen...and it was *magnificent*.

⚜

Keir Wright might be even more handsome than her lust-fuddled mind remembered; time and primitive living adding a rawness to his features and silver-seasoning to that long black hair...but he was also the most vexing man in Scotland.

How could she have thought, even for a moment, that he might return to the village and claim her? Keir didn't want the equally seasoned woman who had come to tend him, he desired a fresh-faced virgin. No doubt some wild Highland lass with lovely green eyes and a fertile womb.

Wishing she had her pestle and mortar so she could crush something to dust, Maude marched to the sideboard that served as his kitchen. The rising sun was already brightening the dwelling through the east window, but she didn't stop and admire a view of rugged, icy-topped peaks that stretched as far as the eye could see. No, she had white willow bark tea to prepare. The sooner Keir was better, the sooner she could flee this place and not think of the man again.

I would not touch the laird's mother.

Bah. It was humiliating enough that she'd blatantly offered herself to Keir, only to discover he wanted someone else. But to be rejected a second time because she had a full-grown son...

Barely suppressing a banshee wail, Maude braced both

hands on the rough wooden bench and stared unseeingly at the jar of herbs in front of her.

It truly stung to know she only had herself to blame for this situation.

Napping in a patient's bed, then crawling closer when she'd woken in the night, chilled to the bone because the fire in the hearth was little more than a smolder and she wasn't under any blankets. Allowing, nay, *welcoming* it when Keir had mumbled something about daft wenches and hauled her against his huge, warm *naked* body. When one brawny arm curled across her belly and breasts, she'd just felt so safe. And wanted. How dangerously easy it had been to set aside the fact that they were healer and patient and imagine him as a longtime lover who still considered her his jewel. Then later, with his hard cock pressed against her bottom, his lips sensually tormenting her neck, his fingers beneath her shift and pinching her nipple...the way she'd whimpered and actually pushed his hand between her legs so he might touch her throbbing core. But not even Keir Wright, the man who'd bedded half the women in the Western Highlands, would pleasure her!

I would not touch the laird's mother.

It was a good thing his leg had pained him before he sullied himself with an old crone who was not only a mother, but also soon to be a grandmother. Before she lost her wits entirely and spread her thighs for an injured man in her care.

Ha. Perhaps in a few years she might even believe that.

"I am more than the laird's mother. Or a healer," she bit out, pouring freshly boiled water into a tankard then adding some dried white willow bark with unusual ferocity. "I am a *woman*. I have *needs*."

"Did ye say something, Lady?"

Maude glared across the dwelling at her patient. "You are supposed to be resting."

"I'm in bed, am I not?"

"We both know being in bed does not mean a body is resting."

Unexpectedly, Keir grinned, and handsome became breathtaking. Devilish knave. "Aye. 'Tis true. Rest is only about the third or fourth best thing to do in bed."

After soundly rejecting her, now he thought to tease and charm?

Purgatory pestilence.

"I wouldn't know," she replied tartly, blowing on the tea to cool it down then carrying the tankard over to the bed and handing it to him.

Keir cupped it in his hands but didn't sip. Instead, he studied her. "That is a sad tale."

"Drink your tea."

"I'll drink it meek as a wee lamb in exchange for the answer to a single question."

Maude huffed out a breath. "What?"

"Ye were wed to the laird for twenty-six years. What was it truly like?"

Her jaw dropped in astonishment. Of all the questions in the world, the very last one she'd expected from Keir was something regarding her terrible marriage.

What could she even say?

I only wed the Lord of Glennoe because my guardian wanted me gone and accepted the first offer he received? Donald was a cruel husband and father in public and so much worse in private? That I welcomed every illness or injury, every birth or battle, because it meant time away from him? That neither me nor my son mourn his passing?

"There were happy days," said Maude stiffly. "The first time I held Callum in my arms. The day we found Alastair in the clearing and brought him back to the castle. Every occasion a patient recovered from an ailment or a babe was safely born."

Keir tilted his head. "I didnae ask about the lads, the world knows ye adore them. Nor did I seek an opinion on being clan healer. I asked about marriage to Donald MacIntyre, Lord of Glennoe, and what it was truly like."

"And why should I answer such a personal question?" she snapped, even as she shuddered at how very *English* her voice sounded.

"Because this morning ye showed me another side of Lady Maude MacIntyre. Passionate and bawdy and spirited. It made me wonder...how on earth ye survived marriage to that festering turd of a laird. Was I really so much worse than him? So crude and unlearned and poor in my service that ye couldn't bear to speak to me? To tend me?"

Shock froze her in place, soon followed by bitter resentment. Although Donald had never loved her or shown any respect or affection, he'd demanded constant praise and admiration. And she'd never been able to feign it, not when she was so drawn to another man. So Donald's vengeance had been to forbid her from tending or speaking to Keir, all while he told Keir blatant lies. Her late husband had loved taunting people for his own amusement; when that wasn't enough, threatening, humiliating, or banishing them. Wretched, poisonous man.

Maude hesitated, unsure how to explain, when a flash of movement out the east window caught her eye. If the child wished to spy, she really needed to cover that unruly red hair.

Resolutely swallowing her emotions, she said, "Sorcha is here. I will prepare her breakfast. Drink that tea, I humbly beseech thee."

Keir scowled, but lifted the tankard to his lips and drained it, before handing the tankard back. She returned to the kitchen, just as Sorcha charged through the partially open door, a small eating dagger clutched in her hand.

"Good morning," said Maude, as though that were an everyday occurrence. "Breakfast?"

The child's wary gaze narrowed. "I'm here to see Uncle Keir. If he's better or if ye did witch spells."

"I'm better and resting," said Keir, sitting up further in bed. "The unseelie failed."

Sorcha's shoulders relaxed and she tucked the dagger away. "You're not red. And only a bit sweaty."

"Must have been those dueling snails."

A faint smile appeared on the girl's face. "The healer helped a bit."

Maude swallowed a laugh. High praise indeed. "I'm going to toast some bread and cheese, but there is too much for one person. Would you do me a favor and eat it, Sorcha?"

"I suppose. If ye cannae finish it all. English ladies eat like baby birds."

"Some do. Go wash your face and hands, then sit at the table."

Sorcha sighed heavily and glanced again at Keir. "Lady Maude *always* wants me to wash my face. I washed it yesterday!"

"Aye, but you'll get toasted bread and cheese," he grumbled. "I get naught but willow bark tea."

Maude smiled sweetly. "If you're very, very good, you might get a few bites."

Keir grunted. "Scoop some water out of the rainwater barrel and wash your face, Sorcha. And those muddy hands. I'll make sure she adds enough cheese."

The child skipped outside, and Maude sniffed. "*Adds enough cheese*? Ha. You think this is my first bread-toasting occasion?"

He didn't laugh or return a jest. Merely studied her once

more with those unsettling hazel eyes. "Hard to say. Seemed like ye had some firsts earlier in bed, so maybe there are a great many things you've yet to experience."

Heat scorched across her cheekbones. Vexing man! Who else but Keir Wright would dare say such a thing?

If only it weren't true.

Apart from admiring Keir, she'd been reprimanded by Donald for many other sins—a scholarly son who resembled her and struggled with a sword, the fact they only had one child instead of many. He'd hated the fact she didn't mindlessly worship him or cower when he exploded with temper. Not once had Donald troubled himself with kindness—although to be fair he hadn't been kind to many in the MacIntyre clan, only his sister and her son who was now the MacDonald of Carnoch, and Gavin MacTier, his most favored guard.

Her late husband certainly hadn't cared a whit for his wife's enjoyment in the marital bed. No nuzzling kisses to her neck or skillful preparation to ensure her readiness to receive him. No holding her securely in his arms so she might be warm.

Why did Keir have to remind her? If she could forget their time in the heather bed, then her body wouldn't crave such things. To be held. Touched. *Pleasured.*

Maude cleared her throat. "Wrong. But I forgive you—a man out of his head with fever. Let us not speak of this again."

Lady Maude was a beautiful little *liar*.

Standing there, claiming she knew about pleasure after twenty-six years of marriage to a cruel bastard like Donald MacIntyre.

Unless the stories of her and the king were true? James Stewart was a lusty young bull and reputedly charming.

Keir frowned darkly as he resettled himself in the heather bed. Even the thought of King James knowing what it felt like to suck Maude's velvety nipples until she squirmed, hear her hoarse pleas for more as he licked her pearl, make her spend as he fucked her...ach. If he pondered that, his teeth would grind to powder. Unsurprising, when he'd held a torch for her so long, but now that he'd woken with Maude MacIntyre in his arms, the notion of another man in her bed—and another woman in his—was unbearable.

"Did ye have an understanding with Donald?" he asked abruptly.

The lady's brow furrowed. "About what?"

"Taking lovers."

A storm brewed once more in those violet eyes. "You were Donald's captain of the guards. You knew his temper. What would've happened had I taken a lover."

"Not from the clan," he persisted, yearning for truth between them. "Much higher. A nobleman. Someone the laird tolerated because it gained him favor."

She snorted, then began cutting chunks of buttered bread and generous wedges of cheese. "My husband tolerated no noblemen. He bedded where he pleased but did not grant me the same courtesy. People followed me everywhere, like grim little shadows. Always watching and whispering, those spies..."

"I spied earlier," said Sorcha as she returned inside, palms up to show she'd actually washed them. "Did ye know that?"

Lady Maude's eyes widened. "Never you say."

"It's *true*."

Keir coughed to disguise a laugh at both the healer's feigned astonishment and his niece's smug smile. Sorcha's flame-colored hair could be seen a mile away, her shawl rustled, and she clomped her shoes; only a corpse would be unaware of the bairn's approach. "Dinnae fret, Lady Maude. She's wily. Sits on the stone wall and spies on me when I train, quiet as a mouse."

Sorcha laughed and twirled. "He's always surprised."

Lady Maude nodded gravely and returned to her task. Soon, the heavenly scent of toasting cheese filled the dwelling as she held a small skillet over the fireplace, her hand protected from burns by a bunched rag.

"Ohhhhhh," said Sorcha as she inhaled deeply and licked her lips like she hadn't been fed in a month.

Keir winced. He could have done better than stew or broth each night, toasted bread and cheese was easy enough. Was he the reason the bairn remained so tiny? Burke and Fiona had made caring for Sorcha look easy. As had Lady Maude with her boys. How had they learned what to do?

Soon they each had a plate of bread smothered with golden cheese. After his first bite, Keir's stomach purred with happiness at the taste, and at having solid food rather than willow bark tea. He also grudgingly conceded that the healer knew how to toast properly.

When they'd finished their breakfast, Lady Maude sat back in her chair. "So, Sorcha, what are you doing today? Perhaps find some more fat snails for your uncle's leg?"

His niece nodded. "I can bring some tonight when I come back for supper. But I'm making twig boats and building a rock bridge by the stream with my friend Craig MacTier."

"Gavin's boy?"

"Aye. Craig walks up from the clearing with his grandmother Ida. He's only six summers, but his mother got a new babe that cries and cries so he comes and plays with me every Tuesday. Ida makes fruit cake. We get one piece each."

Keir stayed quiet, hoping to learn more recent information about Craig's mother and father. While Ida was a blunt-speaking Highland elder with silver hair, dark eyes that could halt unruliness at fifty paces, and an admirably practical manner, her son Gavin and daughter-in-law Heather very much kept to themselves and had never set foot up here. On many occasions Ida had grumbled over her son's 'airs' since he'd been named captain of the guards, even more so after the old laird's death. It was strange that Keir had been replaced by someone with much less experience and skill, but perhaps Gavin had matured in the past few years. Perhaps he was now a fine leader and swordsman.

Alas, Sorcha offered nothing further.

"Babies do cry a lot," said Maude, nodding. "And fruit cake is delicious. But a body can get very hungry building twig boats and rock bridges, so take some oatcakes for everyone as well. And sweetmeats. I'll wrap them in a cloth. Now, do you need your hair plaited?"

He blinked at the question, expecting Sorcha to recoil or offer scorn at such a suggestion. Instead, she looked so sad and wistful his heart clenched in his chest.

"Mother combed and plaited my hair," she said in a very small voice. "But no one else knows how."

Lady Maude tapped her chin. "Perhaps I could try. My plaiting won't be as good as your mother's, but it will keep your hair back when you're building."

"Who will do it when ye return to the castle, though?" asked Sorcha worriedly, biting her lip.

"Me," blurted Keir.

Both stared at him, Lady Maude's eyes wide with genuine astonishment this time, and Sorcha's with an expression he'd not seen since before the raid. Hope.

"Really, Uncle?" she said tentatively. "Plaiting?"

"Oh aye," he said, utterly unwilling to cloud over a small ray of sunshine. Besides, how hard could it be? "But let the lady attend ye now. She might need practice."

Soon, Sorcha's hair was tamed into a neat plait, and she had a parcel of oatcakes and sweetmeats for her outing. Not long after, Craig bounded up the steps like an unbroken colt to fetch Sorcha, his grandmother trailing behind. The elder politely greeted Lady Maude, but her smile to him was warm. Unlike the rest of the village, Ida MacTier cared little for banishment rules.

"She likes you," said Lady Maude hesitantly, when the trio had departed for the shallow mountain stream about a quarter mile away. "I'm surprised Ida hasn't dragged you and Sorcha back to the village."

Keir shrugged and traced a pattern on the linen sheet covering him. "I was banished at the old laird's command; the new laird hasn't reversed it."

"He did! Callum invited you back."

He bloody well did not.

"I've received no such word," Keir replied, careful not to accuse anyone of lying.

Lady Maude frowned; not even that marred her beauty. "Something is amiss here. My son sent Gavin twice, and wonders why you refuse. Do you really wish to live on the mountain rather than in the village?"

"Look around, lady," Keir said irritably. "I live in a hovel, trade with travelers, and keep my sword arm strong fighting sacks stuffed with straw. I'm alone apart from a broken bairn next door. What do ye think?"

For an endless moment, those violet eyes pierced his soul. "You've been wronged. And Sorcha...she is sad, confused, and angry at losing her mother and father. So very angry. She tries to be gruff and stoic like you, so you'll keep caring for her. But she's a little girl who craves love."

Then the healer blinked and pressed her fingertips to her forehead.

Stunned, he could only stare. That voice she'd just used!

Unnaturally calm and flat, like she recited another's words. Had the lady experienced a vision? He'd heard about this gift, but not personally witnessed it before. How shameful others called her witch. No darkness resided in her, no malice. Only a glow of heavenly power and a heart to serve.

"Are ye well?" he asked softly.

Lady Maude nodded, straightening her shoulders like a warrior about to charge into battle. "Can you plait?"

Keir sighed. "Not even a little."

"Then you must learn," she replied, marching over to the bed and perching on the side directly in front of him, before dropping a wooden comb onto his lap. "First remove any knots or burrs from my hair. Go."

Ignoring the command, Keir reverently stroked the mass of white-blond tresses. Certainly a crown of moonbeams, softer than satin and fragranced with lemons. "Such fine hair."

"You should be plaiting, not playing," she whispered, even as her head lolled a little, arching her back and revealing the imprint of hard nipples against her tunic.

"Should I?" he mused, emboldened. "I'd rather play."

"And do what?"

"This." Keir lightly massaged Lady Maude's scalp until she whimpered. As it had earlier, the sound hardened his cock to stone.

"Just that?"

"So much more. I couldn't possibly tell ye though. Far too crude."

"I...I did say *cock* before."

His lips twitched as he firmed the massage. "Indeed. I think ye have a bawdy heart."

Lady Maude began to pant. "Tell me then."

"Verra well. Playing. Hmmm. Imagine a lock of hair teasing those swollen nipples. Or your plait wrapped around my fist and tugged until the scalp prickle made your cunt gush honey."

She turned, gasping. "But you said you wouldn't touch the laird's mother. That you want a virgin!"

Keir sighed. He was indeed a fool to have spoken in haste. "When I first awoke, I thought I was back in the village with a wench. And I wanted her to be Lady Maude MacIntyre verra badly, so I kept my eyes shut. Ye were so shy...I thought it was a bedding game. Then my leg pained me and I realized who ye were...I thought I'd touched ye without permission."

"No. I wanted it," she said unsteadily. "All through the despair of my marriage I often imagined how your touch might feel. This morning I had a taste."

He swallowed hard as emotions coursed through him; lust and need bound together with shock that during those endless years she'd wanted him too. "And now, Maude? Now ye have had a taste?"

Maude trembled, her cheeks pink. "I want more. Everything that was forbidden to me."

Keir nodded slowly. "Then let us make a bargain. Plaiting lessons for pleasure. And dinnae fret about my leg, either. It's my tongue and fingers you'll be riding. If ye care to."

CHAPTER 3

It's my tongue and fingers you'll be riding. If ye care to.

Maude took several deep breaths, but there was no calming herself now, no room in her head for reasons why bedding Keir Wright might be a bad idea. Her whole body craved his touch once more, without misunderstandings or shyness. He, a seasoned bachelor, had made an offer. She, a pleasure-starved widow, had accepted. Now they could be as lusty and carnal and uninhibited in the privacy of this isolated dwelling as they wished.

Such *freedom* after a marriage that had tested her faith at every turn!

Moaning, Maude pressed her thighs together against a burgeoning ache. "Yes. Please. I want all of that."

"Will ye undress for me?" said Keir, his hot gaze already stripping her bare. "I've a fierce hunger to see every inch of your beautiful body."

She hesitated. "You are aware I am forty-two summers and not some pert-breasted village virgin? That in autumn I shall be a *grandmother*?"

Surprisingly, he glared at her. "I am forty-five summers,

with silver in my hair and bones that dinnae like the cold. It's daft to think I'd prefer a young lass when I've waited over half my life for this—"

"That is a long time."

"Twenty-six years is a bloody long time."

"What?" Maude asked, her heart thundering. "But... that's how long you've known me. Since I came to Glennoe as Donald's bride after the tourney in England..."

"Aye," he growled. "An endless curse, knowing ye belonged to another. Every day, desperate to have your taste in my mouth, hear your moans in my ear, feel your nails rake my back."

"Donald forbade me to speak to you," she burst out. "To tend you. It was the cruelest punishment, both as a healer and a woman desperately unhappy in her marriage. But my desire never waned, it only grew stronger, and I prayed every morning for freedom. That one day I might know how it felt to be in your arms..."

Keir took her hand and brushed his lips across her knuckles, the heat of his mouth like a brand. Marking her. "Then take that damned tunic off so I can see the plump breast I held in my hand. The nipple that stabbed my palm. The soft belly I stroked and that thick bush guarding your cunt. Show me *now*."

Maude quivered. No pretty lies here. It wasn't any woman he wanted, it was her.

And she wanted him.

"Another clause to the bargain, Keir," she said unsteadily, running a finger along the square bodice of her tunic. "I'll take this off if you remove your shirt so I can see that fine chest once more."

The garment was over his head and tossed away before she could blink. He possessed a splendid chest with a generous dusting of crisp black hair. Would it be soft or scratchy against her breasts?

"There," said Keir, also loosening the laces of his hose so she could see the equally dark hair at his groin but not the bulge of his cock below. "Now remove that tunic. Quickly. No teasing."

A lightness filled her then, a foolish giddiness like she was sixteen summers again and full of hope for the future. Maude bit her lip against a wayward smile as she knelt on the bed and slowly...so, so slowly...grasped the hems of her tunic and shift, pulling them up as far as her thighs. "It's just so difficult for a lady to get undressed."

"I'll tear the tunic off," he said, his voice low and gravelly. "And your shift."

"Dear me," she murmured in delight, lifting the hem a few more inches. To be desired like this was a balm to the soul, and to know that nothing but pleasure awaited her...paradise. "So *impatient*."

Keir's guttural snarl surrounded her, hardening her nipples so the bodice was rougher than sackcloth against them. Between her legs, there was a desperate pulsing. "Fair warning, lady. The longer ye torment me, the longer I'll make ye wait for release. And that will seem like forever when your nipples ache from being pinched so hard and that swollen little bud between your thighs is throbbing, but I'll not grant ye my mouth."

Maude gasped at the raw, lusty words. The way he just *said* whatever he thought, whatever he wished to do, in the simplest and crudest of terms...well, he'd been correct in suggesting she had a bawdy heart. How refreshing it was, after a lifetime of court and clan intrigues, after the bold lies and false promises of people who swayed with the wind so they might remain in favor. Keir didn't sway. He was hewn rock. No one had to guess his mind.

She removed her clothing. "There. Happy now?"

"Alas not," Keir rasped. "My old eyes cannae see properly. You'll have to come closer, right here on my lap."

"Poor, poor ancient man," she replied, her lips twitching. Then, careful to avoid his injured lower leg beneath the sheet, Maude arranged herself in front of him, one knee each side of his hard thighs. It was a decadent pose, with her legs spread so wide she was forced to balance her hands on his brawny shoulders, leaving her entire front exposed. While being naked did not bother her in the least—she always prayed to the heavens thus—her belly fluttered at the unknown of being in bed with only the second man of her life. "What are you going to do next?"

Keir licked his lips. "Explore every inch. But ye must make me one promise. If there is something ye dinnae like, a place not to be touched, if ye need harder or softer or something different...tell me at once."

"I do so swear," she whispered, both soothed and excited at the words. He promised pleasure like she'd never known, but equally wondrous...he offered choice.

"Then kiss me, Maude."

Leaning forward, she brushed her mouth against his, softly at first then with more firmness as he gripped her hips in his huge hands. When she flicked the tip of her tongue against his lips, demanding entry, he groaned. But soon the sound of her needy whimpers echoed in the dwelling as his hands moved and his strong thumbs found her taut nipples. He circled them to start, then lightly pinched them with the help of his forefingers.

"Harder," Maude gasped between long, sensual kisses that twined their tongues together. A part of her wished they could kiss all day, but the rest of her body craved that talented mouth, the scratch of his beard that made her skin tingle. "Please pinch them harder."

"So pale a pink, like a seashell," said Keir, as he lazily plucked her aching nipples, pulling and tugging them with exquisite firmness. "I wonder if I could turn them into rubies."

She moaned, desperately wanting to touch herself, but unwilling to risk losing her balance by moving her hands from his shoulders. What if he ceased this delicious play? That would be utterly heartbreaking. "Suck my nipples."

His hands fell away. "Beg pardon?"

At the stern tone, wetness trickled down her inner thighs. "Please suck them."

"Better," he replied, resuming his ministrations with rhythmic pinches hard enough to call forth a desperate cry from her lips. It was too much—her nipples were a dusky rose color now—and yet not nearly enough.

"Keir. I need your mouth. And...and to be stroked between my legs. *Please*."

He nodded, yet in retribution for her earlier teasing, the vexing man proceeded to lick her nipples and gently blow on them, while one blunt finger traced a pattern on her inner thighs that parted her bush but maddeningly avoided her throbbing, drenched core.

It was unendurable.

"*Keir*," she begged, her voice breaking.

"Dinnae fret, angel," he soothed. "I'll give ye what ye need."

Moments later, his hot mouth engulfed one nipple. The rough suckling of the tender peak was so good, so utterly necessary that she cried out with joy, but there was far better to come as the finger between her legs rose to part the delicate petals of flesh and ease inside her channel. Soon, she was a mewling mess as Keir penetrated her with a second finger and his thumb teased her swollen, aching pearl, her entire world reduced to a delicious rhythm: in, out, press. In, out, press. Maude writhed at the burst of sensation but Keir gave no quarter, his mouth becoming even rougher on her nipples and his fingers plunging deeper inside her. Then his free hand curved behind her back, coiling her hair around his fist and tugging hard.

Saints alive.

Something wild and urgent took control of her body, sending it hurtling toward pleasure. Maude bucked, her nails clawing his shoulders, her mound grinding against his palm... and abruptly she was there, an untamed cry tearing from her throat as release pounded her like storm waves on a rocky shoreline, the spasms lasting and lasting.

Eventually she slumped against Keir's shoulder, her breath coming in short, panting gasps. "That was...that was..."

"Just the beginning. You've had my fingers, next you'll know how it feels to have my tongue inside ye. I'm going to lie down. You'll straddle my face. And then, my lady, I'm going to feast on that sweet cunt 'til ye scream."

৩৵৩

He'd brought Maude MacIntyre to a powerful release, and Keir wanted to roar his triumph like a lion.

As wife of the laird, she'd been forced to hide her true nature, deny her desires to appease a husband spawned by the devil himself. But here in this dwelling, Maude had shown him glimpses of the passionate, bawdy, spirited woman she was. Now he'd seen her in her full glory; it was clear hours of pleasuring would be required before she was sated. The moans and whimpers of unashamed desire Maude had made as he attended to her! Nothing had ever aroused him more, apart from the musky scent of her soaked center demanding he taste immediately. Aye, he needed to get his tongue inside her without delay, before his cock exploded and ruined another pair of hose.

"Could you help me sit?" whispered Maude, her cheeks flushed. "I feel...unsteady."

Keir swallowed hard. She felt unsteady? Hell, he was more eager than a green lad about to fuck his first lass. Then again, in some ways it was like a first time. All the wenches he'd bedded in the past had been pretty and jolly, and they'd had grand fun together...but his heart had never been involved. With Maude, the need to master her, pleasure her senseless, etch himself upon her soul so she would never crave another...was like a fever inside him that no tea or tonic could quench.

"Aye," he said gruffly. "Up on your knees, let me slide down further so I'm lying flat...there we go. Clever lass. Now put your hands on the headboard, thighs either side of my head. Mmmm, I cannae wait to taste your cunt. The scent of it! I could inhale naught else for the rest of my days and be well satisfied."

She smiled while awkwardly arranging herself, tormenting him as the crisp hair of her bush grazed his bearded jaw. "You really like it? Something so...ah...earthy?"

"I love it. But I need that nectar in my mouth," he replied, his hands gripping her ample arse so he could guide her at will. Then, like a lost man finding his village at last, Keir nuzzled against her bush to part the hair and discover the soft, silken flesh beneath.

So hot. So wet. So ready to be plundered.

Maude trembled, her breathing ragged. "Do it. Taste me. *Please.*"

Slowly, so he might savor it, he dragged his tongue from her back entrance up to her swollen, dark pink pearl, groaning as her sweetness filled his mouth and set his senses ablaze. Aye, he'd waited half a lifetime, but this was worth every cold, endless day.

She cried out, her hips writhing.

However, his hold was too secure and Keir settled into feast, his tongue lashing her pearl before retreating to delve into the heated slickness of her cunt, collecting as much of the honey as he could. She was so open, it trickled onto his cheeks and chin. "Paradise," he said. "I'll not ever have my fill."

Maude sobbed a little, her hips circling and circling as she attempted to get closer, to grind herself against his face. "N-never?"

"Never," he replied firmly, shoving his tongue deep and squeezing her arse to let her know who she belonged to, even brushing her tight rosette with his fingertips.

She gasped. "Keir..."

He paused and tipped his head back, wanting to gauge her true reaction to the caress in a place many deemed forbidden. Did she know of the pleasures to be had with a finger or cock deep in her arse? Was she interested in such play, or was that a step too far for a highborn English lady, even a passionate one?

"Maude?" he said, boldly meeting her gaze.

Her violet eyes narrowed. "You know what."

Keir stifled a smile at the lady of the castle tone. He was always willing to discuss or discard an idea, but never would he dance around the topic like a sly courtier. "Speak plainly, madam. I'm a simple Highland swordsman, after all. Cannae read your learned mind."

Maude's hips moved restlessly. "You touched me."

"In many places, aye."

"My *bottom*."

"Here?" asked Keir, gently stroking her back entrance once again. "Do ye like it, or no?"

She shuddered, and more moisture dripped onto his chin. "I've not been touched there before. It is...strange."

Once again, he felt a sense of triumph. Another first for Maude. He could introduce her to this, teach her more wicked acts that would appeal to a bold and bawdy lover.

"It is new," said Keir. "Everything new is strange at first. But some people greatly enjoy arse play. Once properly prepared, of course, for it is a tight space for finger or cock. I understand it enhances pleasure. Makes a woman spend harder to be filled in two holes at once."

Maude bit her lip. "Perhaps...just a little of your finger to try? While you're, ah—"

"Kissing your cunt? As ye desire. Lift up a bit so I can wet my finger first, there ye go."

Wanting to heighten Maude's arousal once more, Keir stroked between her legs and delved inside her channel to coat his finger in her wetness. Then, languidly licking her pearl the entire time, he returned his finger to her rosette, gently pressing against the tight hole until it surrendered and allowed entry to just the tip.

She made a raw, needy sound, half-moan, half-wail, and he almost did ruin his hose. Was there anything better than a hot-blooded lady finally unleashing the shackles of a bad marriage bed? It was just as well there were no others about.

"More," Maude said thickly. "More tongue. More finger. More, more, *more*."

"Demanding wench," he teased, even as he sank his finger deeper into her arse and fluttered his tongue against her pearl.

Now she rocked, moaning, begging, grinding against his chin, a woman thinking only of release. With a low growl, Keir finger-fucked her arse and plunged his tongue inside her cunt as far as it could go, lapping and rubbing until Maude tossed her head back, screaming his name. All he could do was swallow her gushing honey, take the pressure of her thighs against his ears and her mound sealing his mouth...but by God, if the unseelie took him now, he would go to purgatory a contented man.

Abruptly Keir could breathe again. He gulped several lungfuls of air before turning to see Maude lying beside him in the bed, her gaze soft and sated, her smile like sunshine.

"I could not ride anymore, my knees were starting to hurt," she admitted ruefully. "Yet I've never felt more alive. I mean...I always knew there was so much more to bedding than what I experienced. But that was beyond my imagination. You have a gift. You should *teach* at a university. St. Andrews...Glasgow..."

Laughter rumbled in his chest, and he licked his lips for another taste of the finest cunt in Scotland. "Oh aye, every university should have a Master of Pleasure. As for your knees, I'd offer pity, but the only malady on my mind at present is—"

"A cut leg?"

"Nae. A stone-hard cock. Ye dinnae mind if I attend to it? Won't take long."

"Let me."

Keir hesitated, even as his shaft throbbed with want. "The bargain was pleasure for a plaiting lesson."

Maude slid down the bed and draped herself over his thigh, then had the boldness to *pout* at him. "But I want to taste you. Lick and suck until you spend in my mouth."

Wicked, wicked woman.

"Verra well. Go on, then."

Her hands were clumsy in their eagerness to free his cock from the confines of the hose, but her indrawn breath at the size and thickness revealed made him prideful indeed. Aye, his cock was as large as the rest of him.

At the first touch of her pink tongue to the swollen head, Keir swore.

"Such language in front of the laird's mother," she chided, her eyes glinting with mischief.

"Less talking. More tasting."

"Oh aye," Maude replied, imitating his usual growl. Then she giggled, the sound so free and joyous, he couldn't help smiling in return. The lady had endured far too much darkness in her life.

However, when her pale, slender fingers gripped his length and she took the head of his cock into her mouth and sucked, his hands nearly tore the linen sheet as his hips raised an entire inch off the bed.

"Like that, angel. Just like that."

Except then she took him a few inches deeper, her lips and tongue and the inside of her cheeks all working together in a way that was nothing short of glorious. Keir groaned, sweat bathing his temples as he valiantly attempted to hold off the violent release brewing. But it felt far, far too good. His seed erupted in harsh, wracking jets, and the greedy woman gulped it down like the finest wine until not a drop remained.

God's blood. He'd never believed in miracles, but Maude MacIntyre in his bed truly seemed like a glimpse of heaven.

What a difference an hour could make.

Maude lay sprawled on the heather bed, her head resting on Keir's thigh, and yet her soul practically danced about the room. While she was weary and a little sore—her nipples raw, back entrance mildly stretched where his finger had plundered, legs cramped from kneeling, and her jaw aching after having such a thick cock in her mouth—already she craved him again, because being pleasured by Keir was all the light and joy of a thousand sunbeams.

When his hand began massaging her scalp, she butted against him like a kitten, demanding more.

"Fair warning," Maude said softly, "I will purr."

He shrugged. "A lady should purr. If her lover is doing right by her."

Adjusting herself so she could look up at him, Maude added lightly, "You know...if you ever wanted to do this again, I would very much like that."

Keir's fingers tightened in her hair, the slight tug and subsequent prickle making her pearl throb. How did he *do* that? Turn a little pain into delicious pleasure?

"Maude," he said patiently. "Not even old Henry's entire northern army could stop me wanting to do that again with ye. And again and again after that. I dinnae ken the dwelling we'll be in, but whether in bed, against a wall, spread out over a table or sitting in a chair...one of us will be riding the other. And if anyone in the clan has words to say about that, they can meet my sword. I've waited too long to see ye walk away after one day. Although...if ye fetched some small ale, I could watch that fine arse sway and those perfect breasts bob on the way back."

A hot blush spread across her cheekbones at both the blunt, possessive words and fierce lust in his gaze. "Oh? May I do so, my lord? Perhaps some sweetmeats as well?"

"Always," said Keir. "And 'tis pleasing to hear ye address me so respectfully...here now, no pinching or you'll be on your back and stuffed full of cock."

"Ha!" she replied, both flustered and delighted at the banter. "A likely story with that leg. And may I remind you that my hair remains unplaited."

He sighed heavily. "Verra well. I'll set aside the thought of fucking and accept some small ale for my thirst before I master the art of arranging hair."

Maude sniffed as she climbed off the bed and wandered to the kitchen sideboard to fetch some tankards of small ale and her herb satchel. The white willow bark tea he'd taken earlier was doing a sterling job in easing his pain and fever, but she needed to keep a watchful gaze on that wound site. Although she'd thoroughly cleaned and treated it, and offered up chants, cuts could be devilishly contrary: better one day, festering the next. They required constant inspection.

Before returning to the bed, she also stoked the fire in the hearth, and soon the dwelling was pleasantly warm. A good thing when one wore nary a stitch of clothing.

"I really should get dressed," she mused, handing Keir a tankard.

"A few more minutes for the sake of a poor, injured patient? The comforting sight of those pink nipples might be the difference between life and death. If ye cover up and I perish...what a weight to have on your mortal soul."

Her lips twitched madly at such blather. "Storytelling is a family trait, I see."

"What? I speak only the truth. But if we're talking family...can I ask, did ye only want to birth one child? Or could ye have no more? The way ye were with the laird and Alastair as lads...and now young Sorcha. So verra kind."

The question scraped at her heart, so Maude quickly took a sip of small ale. The beverage was more bitter than she liked, so she added honey to sweeten it from the jar in her satchel. "That is a little hard to explain. Callum's birth was long and difficult, even though he wasn't a large babe. Feet first, you see. My son had to be turned by the midwife and that is a terrible process. But I recovered and marital visits resumed. As much as I loathed Donald, I would have welcomed more children."

"It just didn't happen?"

"No. Not even a missed menses. Donald was furious, and often accused me of taking pennyroyal to prevent conceiving. But I never, ever would. It was such a difficult time...a healer unable to explain why her womb became barren. Nor did I receive any heavenly guidance. My visions are only for others. I've never seen anything for myself."

Keir nodded slowly. "I dinnae envy the burdens of a high-born wife. Having sheets examined, being followed to the privy or blamed if aught goes amiss. How did ye bear it?"

"I helped deliver other children. And rescued an abandoned one," she said with a fond smile. "Finding Alastair helped heal my heart. And Callum's, too."

"Donald accepted that?"

"No. Not ever. He hated me for it. Especially with Callum being scholar rather than warrior, and both my boys copying the way I speak. They don't even sound Scottish! My husband wanted a son like Rory."

Unexpectedly, Keir grinned. "I always loved that ye called the MacDonald of Carnoch *Rory* when he hates the name so much. They were two peas in a putrid pod, Donald and his nephew."

Maude winked. "They were indeed. I adore my peaceful, steady Callum, but knowing he defeated his bullish cousin in the royal tourney to win Isla's hand...how I would have loved to witness Callum raise his longsword and yell *Cruachan* in victory. Oh dear. I truly am a bloodthirsty English witch after all."

"Nae. Just a loving mother."

"And you? No urge to be a father?" she asked tentatively.

Keir set down his empty tankard. "Not really. I was always verra careful where I spilled my seed. But I liked being an uncle when Burke and Fiona were here. I want that again, to be better, even. With Sorcha, well, if I'm confessing, bairns in general baffle me. Her mother and father...and ye...made it look so easy."

Maude nearly laughed at that. *Easy?* Saints alive. "Never easy. Children are baffling to everyone, believe me. We just muddle through as best we can, and try not to howl too much in public. Little ones can stomp on your last nerve, but then they turn around, smile like cherubs, and say I love you, Mother, and you refrain from dropping them in a thistle patch. I'm happy that you want to be a better uncle to Sorcha, poor mite. Those cursed Campbells..."

Just for a moment, an expression of unspeakable rage and grief crossed his face. "Aye. That raid...if I'd been near the weaving house instead of up here...but I chose to break the laird's nose, and that is my burden to bear."

She winced at the reminder. Donald's petty vengeance had resulted in far-reaching consequences: depriving the clan of their best swordfighter when the Campbells had raided and razed the weaving house to the ground. Several had died, including Sorcha's mother and father. As a soothsayer and healer, to have received no warning nor be able to save such good people, had been devastating.

"I always wondered what happened before that punch," said Maude. "I know my husband kept you close for your excellent sword arm, but the two of you were oil and water."

"We were arguing."

"Over what?"

Keir hesitated and rubbed a hand across his bearded jaw. "Does it matter?"

"You need not protect me from anything. I know exactly the man my husband was. Someone who threatened his own son if I did not do his bidding, for he had another heir in his nephew."

He scowled. "Bastard."

"Tell me. Why were you banished?"

"Donald knew I wanted ye. Taunted me all the time, what he'd said or done to ye. But one day...he was in the blackest of moods. Said he was tired of me gazing upon his wife and her gazing upon me and it was time to settle the matter. He gave me a choice. Fight him or he'd harm ye and claim it was an accident. So I broke his nose. Aye, it was satisfying. But after that he had a reason to banish me: an *unprovoked attack*."

Horrified to the core, Maude could only gape.

Everything he'd lost...because of her.

"Oh Keir," she breathed. "No."

"You're shivering," he said, looking away. "Get dressed and we can begin that plaiting lesson before Sorcha returns."

Ah. He did not wish to discuss the matter at all.

Stung at the dismissal, especially after the intense pleasure and playful banter, Maude reluctantly collected her fresh shift and tunic and dressed. Keir also put his shirt back on and retied his hose, before patting the edge of the bed.

She perched in front of him for the second time. "Do you remember the first step?"

"Aye. Comb out the knots and burrs. Then what?"

"Evenly part my hair into three. Take the left section, cross it over the middle section, and pull tight. Then the right section over the middle and pull tight. And so on. It sounds simple, but can be tricky to start. My boys took weeks to learn the skill, and many harsh words were muttered."

"Well, if the laird and Alastair can master it, I can certainly try. For Sorcha."

Maude smiled briefly at the determination in his voice but his hands were almost impersonal now, no gentle stroking or lusty tugging or soothing massage. And she *missed* the intimacy.

How could she get that back?

And how could she convince a stubborn, grieving High-lander to lower his walls and let her in?

CHAPTER 4

Lady Maude MacIntyre tied him up in knots. Much like his bloody plaiting.

Keir glared at the length of linen bandage in his hand. Maude had cut a piece from the roll and split it into three so he could practice, after sitting patiently for at least an hour while he fumbled with her hair. It wasn't going well; his attempts weren't a neat plait, more a crooked worm with a distended belly crawling across the sheet. Much like caring for a child, plaiting looked easy yet made a body want to howl.

At the present time, she was serenely treating his leg. At least it wasn't cobwebs and snails; that had been a slimy, tickling sensation he had no desire to repeat. On the other hand, his leg was so much better—the sickening throbbing reduced to a dull ache—it was hard to compare the two days against each other. Yesterday, in his pain and fever, purgatory had seemed mere steps away. Right now, lying on a soft heather bed with each of the dwelling's three window shutters open to allow in weak rays of sunshine and a fresh mountain breeze, he felt good. Surprisingly so.

Perhaps that was just the aftermath of some wickedly lusty play with the woman he'd wanted half his damned life. To bring her pleasure, taste her on his tongue, hear his name screamed as she writhed in release, then to spend in her mouth...it was hard to imagine anything better. Except having her over and over, and how could they possibly do that if she returned to the castle and resumed her old life? Had anything changed for her after their bedsport, or would he once again find himself defeated by those with noble blood?

Keir cleared his throat. "So, what is your learned opinion on my leg? Safe or no?"

Maude glanced up from where she was generously smearing a vibrant purple-colored concoction onto his skin. At least coneflower salve smelled better than it looked. "I am always cautious with cuts; when people are too confident too soon, they often pay dearly for it. But I'm pleased with progress so far. Your leg is responding very well to treatment."

"Ye truly have a gift."

"Thank you," she replied, smiling briefly. "I must say, it is most agreeable to treat someone who doesn't wish to argue my methods. That can be wearying."

Argue? Why would anyone be that daft when her methods were so successful? In truth, her skill in the art of healing was nothing short of astonishing.

He couldn't master *plaiting*. Or even talk about past hurts.

Keir rubbed his jaw. Lack of robust conversation up here on the mountain had worsened his manners, and put an unnecessary wall between him and Maude. He should have welcomed her compassion, not brushed it aside. And also reassured her that in no way did he hold her responsible for his actions, that of her husband, or the wretched Campbells. Everyone had made choices. The consequences for that were his alone.

He did miss his brother and sister-in-law terribly, though.

Especially the banter between Burke and himself as they hunted together or built a structure. Little things like Fiona chasing him with her embroidery shears when she thought his hair grew overlong, or the way she'd teased him about his procession of wenches while she scrubbed pots or thumped bread dough. He missed all the well-cooked food they'd eaten together; that chorus of taps as wooden spoons dug into wooden bowls at the kitchen table amongst the constant chatter. What he wouldn't give to hear that kind of noise again each day. Sometimes the silence here on the mountain, only broken by the lonely whistle of the wind outside, was suffocating.

"I've no doubt it would be wearying," he said eventually. "Not much longer though, and ye can escape back to the castle. I'm sure there are many in the clan cursing my name for taking ye away."

"You are part of the clan and therefore also entitled to my help," Maude replied, adding more purple salve to his leg. God's blood, it looked horrific. Like something even the unseelie would fear.

"The laird truly wishes me to return?"

"He does. And I shall inform him that Gavin disobeyed the order to invite you back. Twice. I hope he has a good reason, because I certainly cannot think of one. Well, apart from protecting his own position. But that is entirely selfish, not putting the good of the clan first. We need you...but beyond that, *I* need you," she finished softly.

Keir sucked in a breath as hope soared within him. "Maude—"

The sound of clomping shoes on the steps distracted him, then Sorcha and Craig raced through the door, the lad's grandmother trudging wearily behind them.

"Good afternoon," said Maude. "How fare the builders?"

"Verra well!" said Craig, his gaze darting about the room. "Keir, your leg is *purple*! Does it hurt? Will it fall off?"

"Hush, laddie," scolded his grandmother. "Dinnae be bothering Lady Maude."

"Your grandson may always ask me questions, Ida," said Maude politely, as she wrapped Keir's leg in a fresh linen bandage. "I'm also delighted you are both friendly with my patient. When I arrived to treat his wound, I brought the laird's best regards. He holds no ill-will toward Keir and warmly welcomes his return to the village."

Keir blinked in surprise at the announcement. Word would spread quickly once Ida returned home and told her family and those who lived nearby. Everyone in Glennoe knew of the bad blood between him and the old laird; Maude had just made it very clear the new laird considered the matter done.

Ida MacTier looked equally stunned, but soon gathered herself. "Long past time. I never like to speak ill of the dead, but the banishment was even more foolish than a healer not tending the captain of the guards. Well. 'Tis pleasing you've kept your sword arm strong, Keir. Lady Isla needs help training the warriors now she has a babe in her belly. Ach, those Sutherland guards of hers. Who really knows if they can be trusted? I keep one hand on my coin purse when passing by."

He almost laughed. If there were two things an elder could say to reassure him that she fully accepted the new laird's decree, it was praise for his sword arm and complaints about another clan. Although here they were unfounded—part of Lady Isla's dowry in her marriage to the laird had been fighting men from her powerful father's guard. They were utterly loyal to the Lady of Glennoe, who was in turn utterly loyal to her husband and lover.

"'Tis good to be cautious, Ida," Keir said mildly.

"Aye, you never know when trouble might strike. Not with Campbells and MacDonalds forever circling. Come along, Craig, we must return home before the storm sets in."

"Storm?" asked Sorcha abruptly. "But...but the sun is shining."

Ida nodded. "I feel it in my bones, lassie. You'll see."

Not long after, the MacTiers left the dwelling to walk back down the mountain path. Keir expected his niece to provide a detailed account of her and Craig's building adventure by the stream, but the bairn was oddly quiet.

"Did ye make a fine rock bridge with Craig?" he asked at last, when the silence stretched too thin for him to bear.

Sorcha shrugged and sat down at the kitchen table. "Fine enough. Craig's not learned everything about building yet."

"Aye. Just an apprentice."

His niece didn't laugh or preen, she drummed her fingers on the table and glanced out the window.

Keir looked helplessly at Maude for guidance. "What do ye think? Six summers for an apprentice, eight summers for a master bridge builder?"

"Certainly," the healer replied. "But I cannot think about building right now. I'm too concerned about the upcoming storm. They frighten me, all that thunder and lightning and rain. Do they frighten you too, Keir?"

He stared at her in utter bewilderment, knowing for a fact she had braved countless storms to tend patients in the village. She stared right back, her head tilting ever so slightly toward Sorcha. Then the infernal woman pinched his toe for good measure.

"Oh aye," Keir croaked. "Hate them. The roof always leaks."

Sorcha sighed. "Suppose I'll have to sleep here tonight, then. So you're not scared."

"That would be very kind," said Maude. "We can walk to

your dwelling and gather your nightgown or anything else you need. Then we'll have some supper."

"Uncle makes good broth."

"It won't have any meat," he warned. "I haven't been out hunting for a few days."

"I'm sure we can make something tasty," said Maude. "Shall we go, Sorcha?"

As he watched them leave, Keir shook his head and lay back on the pillows. How had the lady done that? She barely knew Sorcha, yet had noticed a fear he'd not even realized the bairn endured. He would need to learn far more than plaiting to be a better uncle. Craig MacTier had at least reached apprentice level at building rock bridges, but Keir Wright had significantly further to go as a guardian.

Damn it all.

❦

Keir had broken Donald's nose not because of taunts, but a direct threat against her.

And in his banishment, he'd paid a terrible price.

As Maude walked with a skipping, chattering Sorcha to the dwelling next door, her heart felt heavier than a boulder in her chest. No doubt this was retribution for lusting after a man other than her husband and praying for freedom all those years: the knowledge she had played a part in causing Keir and Sorcha such agonizing pain.

If only she'd been able to hide her attraction to Keir. But that would have asked the moon, the sun, and the stars. And now that she had tended him on this mountain, that she'd had the time and privacy to see beyond his looks and brawn, her ungovernable attraction to him had only grown stronger. For now she had seen the heart of him; that beneath the blunt words, stubbornness, and growling, was a rare man of resolute honesty and loyalty, of gruff kindness and wicked jests.

Ha. Do not forget his tongue...or his fingers...

Maude almost stumbled on the path. As if she could forget pleasure like that. Not even the first taste of a fine wine or rich pastry could compare to a powerful release.

"In here, Lady Maude."

Smiling determinedly, she followed Sorcha into the dwelling. Like Keir's, it was also constructed of stone and clay with three windows and a high thatched roof. However, it was bigger, perhaps several feet wider, and rather than one room, it had three: two bedchambers separate from the kitchen and dining area. There was even a small alcove with a copper tub, an indoor privy, and on a wide bench, what appeared to be the remnants of an herb garden. Her heart broke all over again at the sight of sewn curtains at the windows, woven rugs on the floor, a vase with dried flowers, and a sewing chest. Keir's sparsely furnished dwelling had no air of permanence or love within it. This had been a *home* with a husband and wife who adored each other and their child. No wonder Sorcha didn't want to leave it.

"How beautiful," said Maude wistfully.

Sorcha beamed. "Father and Uncle Keir built it. Mother sewed the blankets and curtains. My special blanket has an S and primroses on it because they are my favorite. I like to sleep with my mother's shawl over my nightgown as well. It's blue and very soft. Do ye want to kiss Uncle Keir? Grandmother Ida thinks so. She said your eyes were shooting love sparks at each other, but I didnae see any."

Maude blinked at the abrupt change in topic, something children took great delight in doing. Then a blush swept across her entire face. Yet again she'd failed to hide her feelings from an audience; canny Ida had seen through her like a pane of glass. "Love sparks? My goodness. What do you think?"

"Maybe. Ye *coo* at each other."

"Coo?" said Maude with a laugh. "Like a pair of pigeons?"

"Aye. And he likes your cheese toasting," Sorcha replied with great dignity. "Father liked Mother's toasting and they kissed all the time."

"Toasting is important."

"What else is important?"

Tapping her chin, Maude considered the question with the gravity it required. Girls deserved so much more than an attractive face or heavy purse. "They must be kind. Not someone who bellows or lies or is prone to whipping. And they should think you are wonderful."

"Even with uncombed hair and muddy shoes?"

"Especially then."

"I don't know who I'll wed," said Sorcha as she gathered up her primrose blanket, nightgown, and blue shawl. "Craig is my friend but he cannae build a rock bridge. Perhaps I'll go to a tourney far, far away like the laird and Master Alastair did to find Lady Isla. Or maybe I'll just sit in a tree and jump into a lad's cart when he drives past. Is one husband better, or two? Two would be a lot of toasting and I burn the bread."

Maude nodded solemnly. "You don't have to decide for a while yet. Perhaps you'll meet a lad you wish to kiss, or two lads, or even a lass. But your heart will guide you at the right time."

The child relaxed further. "That is good. How old were ye when ye wed the laird?"

"Sixteen summers."

"Did ye miss your mother and father when ye left England?"

She winced at the innocent question. As the indulged

daughter of a wealthy knight and his lady love, her childhood had been wonderful. But not long after she'd turned seven, her father, mother, and younger sister had all died in a small plague outbreak and she'd become the ward of a great English baron and his wife. Everything changed. Gone was her life of hugs, chants, and dancing in a sun-drenched apothecary while her mother sang and prepared tonics. Instead, she learned about strict rules and cold piety. Her guardians had been horrified when she started experiencing her 'devilish' visions, wanting her wed and gone as soon as possible. They hadn't cared to whom. Rather foolishly, she'd thought a Scottish laird would mean a life of freedom and adventure. In truth, she'd gone from one prison to another.

"They passed when I was a little girl, even younger than you," said Maude. "I stayed with an English baron. He hosted a tourney and that is where I met the laird."

"Oh. So ye have been sad sometimes," said Sorcha as she hugged her belongings closer to her chest. "Shall we go?"

"I think so," said Maude, grateful the interrogation was over. No one could ask pointed questions like a child, and the past was painful to consider.

She was just about to leave the dwelling when her neck prickled. Halting, Maude stared at the small portrait of Burke and Fiona Wright that sat on a shelf next to the sewing chest. "Who painted that? It's very good."

"A traveler. He bargained a portrait for some food and ale."

Maude's vision clouded briefly, a pulse pounding her temples. *"Take the portrait as well."*

The child stared at her, eyes wide, then snatched it up. "Your voice sounded strange then."

"Forgive me. I have a parched throat in sore need of some wine."

They returned outside and Maude latched the dwelling door, but the prickling feeling did not abate. More than a little uneasy now, she glanced around the quiet, still mountain and up at the sky which was turning an ominous gray. Was it just the impending storm making her feel this way, or something else? How could the home that had seemed so inviting and full of love become a place to flee from, complete with rescued special blanket, shawl, and painted portrait?

Ack. Sometimes her soothsaying gift was plain frustrating.

"I wonder what Uncle is doing," said Sorcha as they approached the front steps of Keir's dwelling.

"Resting, I hope."

The child marched inside. "He's chopping vegetables!"

Maude sighed, closing the door behind her, and the sense of shutting away the outside world improved her mood. "Go and put your belongings on the heather bed. I'll see to your naughty uncle."

Keir turned and scowled at her from the sideboard where he was slicing up a pile of carrots, beans, onions, and leeks with a dagger. "I cannae lie abed all day."

"Yes, you can," she said impatiently. "That is what people do, when they wish to heal an injury."

"It doesnae hurt so much now."

Maude folded her arms and glared at him. "Because you've had enough willow bark tea to launch a ship. The coneflower salve dulls pain as well. That does not mean your leg is ready for battle. I'll chop the vegetables."

"Oh, ye can cook?" he said, raising an eyebrow.

"A little. It's not so different from preparing salves or tonics. But you could sit down and instruct."

"Will ye nag until I do?"

"Yes."

"Ugh, verra well," Keir grumbled, shuffling over to the carved kitchen chair and slumping into it. "There is barley and dried peas in those tins there to thicken the broth."

In the following hours, while both Keir and Sorcha

offered guidance on the correct way to make broth, Maude gained a fresh appreciation for those who toiled in the castle kitchens. She pricked her finger, spilled some dried peas, singed the hem of her tunic, and poured too much water over the broth ingredients. But finally, supper was bubbling in the large pot over the hearth. After adding a sprinkling of bog myrtle to add flavor, she then bustled around the dwelling to light candles as the sun set outside.

A rumble of thunder sounded, and Sorcha flinched.

"Oh dear," said Maude, sinking into the remaining chair next to Keir. "I think the storm is nearly here. There is only one cure I can think of. A good cuddle."

Sorcha stood and moved around the table, then clambered onto Keir's lap and curled her thin arms about his neck. "Dinnae fret, Uncle. I won't let the storm get ye."

Keir's flustered, startled expression at the show of affection from his niece left Maude once again torn between sobbing and laughing, but she gestured for him to pat Sorcha's back as the child nestled her undersized body against his massive chest. In truth, she wanted to join Sorcha and curl against Keir like she had in bed, to once again feel that sense of absolute warmth and security.

Everyone deserved to feel safe, to have a respite from the ills of the world outside.

Even if it was only for a little while.

"Keir, this is an important uncle test, even more so than plaiting. You've managed to get your niece to sleep at a reasonable hour while a storm rages outside...but she is sprawled diagonally across the bed, ensuring no one else may sleep in it. What will you do next?"

He shook his head at Maude's whispered words. This was

certainly a trap. "I dinnae ken how such a wee bairn can take up an entire bed. Like an oversized cat. And she's snoring!" he muttered in reply.

"Snuffling," said Maude generously.

"*Snoring.*"

"So, you're going to wake her up, then?"

Keir grimaced. "Dinnae be daft. We can take those pillows and sleep in chairs in front of the fire. I'm sure ye have done that before. There is another blanket in the chest."

"Well done," she said, her eyes glinting. "You passed the uncle test. Never wake a slumbering child; they'll be both fiendishly irritable and impossible to settle later."

"Sounds more frightening than a storm."

"Oh, it is. By the by, do not dare lift those chairs. I will do that."

He stilled and glared at her, flushing at how easily she'd read his intent. "I lifted ye easily enough."

Maude's cheeks went pink. "You were lying down. And I was holding the headboard. Those chairs aren't going to offer any assistance."

The infernal woman was correct, of course. Grumbling under his breath, Keir fetched the extra blanket while she moved the kitchen chairs to a warm spot in front of the fireplace. Then she deftly removed the bed pillows without disturbing Sorcha, handing him one on her return. A flash of lightning lit up the room followed by a bone-shaking roll of thunder, and he glanced over at his niece. She continued to snore peacefully.

Bairns. They were indeed baffling.

When he and Maude were settled in front of the fireplace's warming golden glow with the blanket shared across their laps, he studied her. "Are ye afraid of storms? Or was that just a kindness to Sorcha?"

"My fright may have been mildly overstated," she replied,

her lips quirking. "Although I do not enjoy reminders of how powerful and destructive nature can be..."

When the healer paused, his brow furrowed. "Maude?"

"I had a vision when we were fetching Sorcha's belongings. That is why she brought the portrait back as well as her blanket and shawl. The moment we stepped outside her dwelling...I felt such *danger*. But I don't know if that was just the strength of the impending storm. Bah...it sounds foolish now—"

"Never that," Keir replied firmly.

Her gaze softened, then she plumped her pillow and rested her head against it. "My visions really don't bother you, do they?"

"Nae. They help people. Will ye sleep now?"

"I might read a little until this storm has passed. At least it's not bringing heavy rain as well."

"That is a boon. I wasnae lying when I said the roof leaks. Did ye bring a book? I have none, alas. Not much of a reader."

"No book, but a letter from the king," she replied with a bright smile, rummaging under the blanket before holding up a square of folded parchment with the royal seal imprinted in wax. "He writes to me twice each month; all the court news and scandals. And his interests, which always change! One day it is architecture, the next shipbuilding, or alchemy or dentistry...James is so clever."

Keir clenched his jaw against a surge of pure jealousy. Of course, the old laird had made no fuss about his wife's long-standing friendship with the king. It was only lowborn, unlearned swordsmen like Keir Wright who had been forbidden to speak to her or dream of something more.

"Verra clever," he said shortly. "Well, I'm tired, might go to sleep now."

"Good night, Keir," she said, even more angel-like than usual with a firelight halo.

"Good night, Maude."

It seemed like he'd barely closed his eyes when his arm was jostled.

"Keir! Wake up."

He blinked, rubbing a hand across his face. The dwelling was still bathed in pre-dawn gloom, but the first tentative rays of morning were seeping through cracks in the walls and around the windows. "Aye?" he replied, sitting up in the chair and flexing his stiff shoulders and neck.

"That noise," Maude whispered. "Do you hear that?"

Keir frowned. Then froze. A faint crackling and popping sound, like something was ablaze...

Tossing away the blanket and hauling himself out of his chair, Keir stifled a curse as his injured leg protested the sudden movement. But he forced himself to continue over to the kitchen to open the wooden shutter and look out the window.

God's blood.

His home was on fire!

For a moment he stared in utter disbelief as sparks whipped about like evil fireflies and the thatched roof that covered the porch began to collapse. Then, directly above him, tiny tendrils of smoke curled their way into the dwelling. His heart seized. In no time at all the entire roof would catch and they would be trapped by falling debris.

"Get Sorcha," he snarled over his shoulder to Maude. "I'll get buckets to put out the fire. We can fill them from the rain barrel."

She nodded and hurried over to the bed where Sorcha was stirring. "Wake up, sweetling. We need to go outside. Hurry now, there's a good girl."

Keir snatched up two wooden buckets and limped to the front door as fast as he could, wincing as the stretch and pull made his wound throb. But when he lifted the latch and pulled it, nothing happened apart from a faint rattle of chains.

Horror filled him. The door had been secured from the outside.

"Keir?"

He looked at Maude, who was carrying a sleepy and clinging Sorcha in her arms. "We cannae go that way. And the windows are shuttered with wood, we won't have time to kick them off before they burn."

She gasped; her eyes wide with frightened understanding.

"Uncle?" said Sorcha tremulously. "What is happening?"

"The big door is a bit stuck, bairn," he said, trying to keep his voice steady as rage clenched his fists. "Dinnae fret though, I have a special door in the floor. Lady Maude will collect your belongings and put them in that sack, there. And she'll get her herb satchel. I'll clear the tunnel, then you'll follow me."

Hobbling over to the south wall, he wrenched aside the wooden chest, revealing a trapdoor he'd installed in the dirt floor because a seasoned warrior always had a secret escape route. It had taken him many weeks to dig the eight-foot-long tunnel and secure it with a wooden frame, but the effort was worth it. The tunnel had another trapdoor outside; the wood covered by a thin layer of dirt that looked like a vegetable patch. No one passing by would know it existed.

After sheathing his sword and daggers, he threw them into the tunnel and climbed in after them. Ignoring the eye-watering agony as he scraped and bumped his wound, Keir shuffled forward on his knees and elbows until he reached the end, then he nudged the second trapdoor up just a few inches to look around. Clear. But the smell of smoke was pungent in the frigid dawn air as he flung the door open and hauled himself and the weapons out into the dirt.

"Maude!" he called. "Both of ye come now."

"I'll send Sorcha first," said Maude. "Go on, sweetling. Be a brave girl."

"I know it's dark," coaxed Keir, his heart pounding relentlessly. "But crawl on all fours like a wee pup. Can ye do that for Uncle?"

Moments later, Sorcha's sack dropped into the hole with a soft thud. Then she moved on her hands and knees toward him, shoving the sack in front of her. Eventually she scrambled up beside him. "Are we fleeing the unseelie?"

"We are," he replied as he waited for Maude to reach him, because whoever had chained the door was pure evil. "Nearly there, Maude. Pass me that satchel, then give me your hand and I'll lift ye out."

When she was above ground as well, Keir faltered in relief, hugging Sorcha before curling his hand around Maude's neck and kissing her fiercely. But they needed to get far away from the dwelling. It would burn swiftly and collapse soon after.

Scooping Sorcha and her sack onto his hip, he awkwardly rose to his feet; the strain on his leg almost making his knees buckle. Then he helped Maude to stand, and after unsheathing his sword in readiness, they walked forward to peer around the side of the wall. But there wasn't a soul about. If it weren't for the thin chains securing the door, he'd have remained unaware of any intruders on his land...perhaps assumed the fire had been sparked by an unfortunate lightning bolt from the storm.

Keir cursed. How had he not heard anything? Surely footsteps or the rattle of chains or the metallic grind of a fire striker?

Maude touched his arm, her gaze troubled. "Willow bark

tea dulls pain and the scent of heather relaxes a body to sleep. There is nothing wrong with your senses…oh!"

Following her shocked gaze, Keir sucked in a harsh breath. He pressed Sorcha's face against his shoulder so she did not see the two words, painted in what looked like pitch, on his west wall. For in the fierce light of the fires consuming both thatched roofs, they were horribly clear.

Traitor. Witch.

His gut roiled. Further evidence that this was no random attack.

Someone had tried to kill him, and Maude and Sorcha as well. As so few people knew they were up here together, the would-be murderer had to be a member of Clan MacIntyre.

God's blood.

CHAPTER 5

As the thick black smoke from the burning dwellings had been easily seen from the village, Maude, Keir, and Sorcha were quickly rescued from the mountain. They hadn't even needed to use the simple yet effective system of flaming distress beacons spaced a mile apart that trailed from one end of MacIntyre land to the other.

Her son said little as he bundled them onto horses and ushered them back to Glennoe Castle with the protection of heavily armed guards. But now Callum's scholarly mind was intent on unravelling the mystery, and he appeared deeply troubled as he stood at his library's thinking window, a spot with usually-soothing views of both Ben Cruachan and Loch Etive.

"So if I understand correctly, Mother, you strongly suspect a member of our clan to be responsible for the attempted murder of yourself, Keir, and young Sorcha, and the destruction of two dwellings. Not a traveler, or small raiding party."

Maude closed her eyes briefly, knowing the hue and cry her answer would raise. But she could only speak the truth. "Two words were painted on the wall. Traitor and Witch.

Only those in the castle and some of the guards knew I was on the mountain tending Keir's injury."

A tense silence fell in the library. Alastair began rubbing Callum's shoulders and Isla poured him a whisky, which Callum drained with a single gulp. Over on a cushioned chaise, Keir sat with a slumbering Sorcha in his lap, the little girl having worn herself out weeping at the loss of her home.

"I'll hunt them down," snarled Alastair abruptly. "They chained the door! That is English cruelty...er, present company excluded, Mother."

"I'm not offended," Maude replied, trying to remain calm when she wanted to pound on every door in the village and shake every person until she had answers. "I know very well what Englishmen are capable of both at home and on foreign soil. However, these crimes were committed by a Scot. Or Scots."

"True," said Isla reluctantly.

"Ye must wait your turn for the hunt though, Alastair," said Keir softly, his hand resting protectively on Sorcha's back. "They tried to kill me and mine."

Maude shivered at the barely-leashed menace. The others might think he referred only to his niece, but she wasn't so sure. That kiss after he'd pulled her free from the tunnel had been so fiercely possessive, she could still feel her lips tingling. And she *wanted* to belong to him, to continue simple joys like waking in his arms, sitting in front of the fireplace and discussing matters, or jesting over toasted bread and cheese. To have a lover who wasn't cowed by her healing or soothsaying, but accepting and encouraging.

"I am particularly concerned they tried to kill a child," added Maude. "One who had already lost so much. Now the last connection with her mother and father has been destroyed."

Keir shook his head. "Sorcha has the portrait, due to your blessed sight."

Callum went still. "You had a vision, Mother?"

She sighed. "A brief one, when Sorcha and I collected some items so she could stay the night in Keir's dwelling with us. It was important to take the portrait. But...I also sensed danger, although I knew not what. Perhaps a warning that the storm would be bad. I certainly did not see fire or a chained door. It is only because Keir is a skilled and experienced warrior who had a secret trapdoor in the floor that we all safely escaped. I owe him my life."

Keir grunted. "We're even, lady. You saved my leg."

"What will we do next?" asked Isla, as she began pacing the library. "This cannot be permitted. The laird's mother, a child, a warrior with a powerful sword arm, all nearly murdered. Fire and destruction! Whoever is responsible must forfeit *everything*. Including their life. I will gladly administer the death blow."

Maude nearly smiled at that. Her swordfighter daughter-in-law was every inch as fierce as any Highland man. "As a healer, I do not wish for anyone's death. But in such terrible circumstances..."

A shudder passed through her, and her eyes stung with unshed tears. The entire time she'd lived in Scotland, it had been made clear to her that she didn't belong. That no matter what she did, how many lives she saved, babes she delivered, or tonics she distributed, there would be those who hated her just because she was born in England and had unusual-colored eyes. But while she might jest about being drowned in the loch as a witch, someone in the clan had decided to go much further and *burn* her; punishing two other innocents as well.

"Ye need to rest, Maude," said Keir gruffly.

"So do you," she shot back. "After crawling through a tunnel, that leg needs more salve."

Isla raised one winged eyebrow. "As Lady of Glennoe, I insist you both rest. I will arrange for the guest chamber next to Mother's to be made up for Keir. I'm sure he will appreciate close proximity to...herbal remedies."

Maude bit her lip and tried not to flush with guilt. Her daughter-in-law had clearly arrived at some accurate conclusions regarding Keir, but mercifully decided to be discreet. The last thing she wanted right now was an exchange of words with Callum and Alastair about events in the privacy of the dwelling, or whether Keir was a suitable companion for the laird's mother. In truth, all she craved was Keir's arms around her, his mouth on hers. What had he said to her in bed? Less talking, more tasting? Such wisdom should be inscribed in stone. "And Sorcha?"

"There is a chaise in that guest chamber. I shall sit with the bairn while you attend to Keir."

Keir nodded, but there was a faint hint of color to his cheeks as he stood, careful not to disturb his niece. "My thanks, lady. Perhaps, laird, we could meet after supper or on the morrow to discuss matters further? I believe we'll all have clearer heads then."

"Of course," said Callum. "I'll post extra guards around the castle. No one will be allowed in or out until I decide otherwise. What occurred today on the mountain is unfathomable. When I think of what could have happened..."

Maude rose to her feet, not wanting to think about that at all. Then she bobbed a curtsy. "Fortunately, it did not. But I appreciate your vigilance, my son. I bid you good day and will see you at supper."

She, Keir, and Isla walked in silence to the guest chamber.

After settling Sorcha on the chaise wrapped in her shawl and the primrose blanket, Keir hesitated. "Are you sure ye dinnae mind, Lady Isla? This won't keep ye from other duties?"

Isla smiled as she leaned back in an overstuffed leather armchair. "If you share this with anyone, I will run you through...but I appreciate the chance to put my feet up in a quiet place. Today this babe is gifting me with a roiling stomach and swollen ankles, and I am rather displeased. Not good sport in the least."

"I can bring you a tonic," offered Maude.

"You just go and tend your man. Er, your patient," said Isla, her eyes gleaming.

Maude and Keir exchanged a furtive glance, but said nothing more as they walked through the adjoining door and closed it behind them.

"My bedchamber," said Maude softly. "The apothecary is in that antechamber over there."

"Lead on."

Usually the powerful scent of herbs, the utter familiarity of the room soothed her senses, but when she attempted to move a pestle and mortar, they dropped from her nerveless fingers onto the oak desk with an overloud clatter. "Purgatory pestilence!"

Keir's hands came to rest on her shoulders, his thumbs massaging her neck. On another occasion she might have purred, but she craved those hands in other, more needy places.

"Maude. Do ye wish to talk about the fire this morning? I know it was a terrible thing."

Certainly not. There had been sufficient talking and thinking. "N-no."

"Tell me what ye need, then," said Keir, the low rumble of his voice dancing across her skin and bringing it to life.

"I need...I need..."

"Aye?"

"I need to *fuck*," she whispered, crude and blunt so there would be no misunderstanding.

Keir inhaled unsteadily. Then he bit the sensitive spot where her neck met her shoulder, making her whimper. "It claws my soul that someone tried to hurt ye this day. I couldnae bear to lose ye, so I'm neither calm nor rational. If ye let me inside that sweet cunt, it won't be gentle, but rough and hard. And once won't be enough. I'll fill ye with seed, angel. Over and over 'til naught remains."

Maude moaned and turned around so she could unfasten the single button on his shirt, eager to feel the heat and strength of his broad bare chest. "I want rough and hard. I need it. Please."

୧୨୨

I need to fuck.

Four words, filled with such aching desperation had heated Keir's blood to boiling point. He could not rest now until he was balls-deep inside Maude's wet heat, until her cries of pleasure near lifted the roof.

Curling an arm about her waist, he lifted her onto the large oak desk. With ruthless purpose, he grasped the bodice of her healer's tunic and tore it, before doing the same with her linen shift, and tossing the ruined garments away. Then, he allowed himself the reward of drinking in Maude's exquisite form. Ah, but she was beautiful. Her hair. Her face. The fullness of her breasts and belly and hips. Her learned mind and skilled hands.

Everything about her, really.

As though she knew her power over him, Maude shoved aside some papers and a leather-bound book, lay back on the wide wooden surface, then braced herself on her elbows and spread her thighs. Her pale pink nipples were taut, and further down, the darker pink flesh peeking through her blond bush was dewy with moisture. Even in a room with so many strong herbal scents, the musky sweetness of her cunt surrounded him like a velvet cloak. Keir's mouth watered to taste her, but he would work his way down.

Leaning forward, he kissed her, holding the back of her neck captive as he twined his tongue with hers to feel even closer, as he bruised her lips with the force of his desire. He wanted her more than anything on earth. Much more than before, because now he'd seen all of Maude. Not just the healer or mother, but also the wise and sensitive soothsayer, the courageous lioness in times of fright, the mischievous jester who bantered and teased and went toe to toe with him...and the bawdy lover who felt just right in his arms.

When she panted for breath, he trailed his mouth downward, kissing her neck and collarbone, lightly scratching the creamy skin of her breasts with his beard before fastening his lips around her right nipple and sucking hard. Maude cried out and tangled her fingers in his hair, an attempt to pull him closer and force more of her breast into his mouth, like the passionate woman she was.

"So sweet," he rasped, flicking the taut peak with his tongue. Then he tugged it with his teeth, batted it lightly like the touch of a butterfly wing, before sucking so roughly her nipple was soon wine-colored. "Will ye spend just from having your nipples pleasured, I wonder?"

"Keir, *please*," she begged hoarsely, her hips bucking as one of his hands crept down to rest on her mound. "Don't make me wait. I cannot bear it."

Keir first tormented her left nipple with the same treatment, flicking and tugging and sucking, then he moved back to issue his command. "Hold your knees to your chest, angel. Show me where ye want my cock."

Maude obeyed instantly, trembling as she offered herself up for a Highlander's plunder. "You know where. Just hurry."

"I cannae hurry," he replied. "Not with such fine honey to be sampled."

Parting her bush, Keir licked her slowly from back entrance to swollen pearl. God's blood, the taste of her! Even headier than the scent.

Merciless in his ministrations, he lapped at her slick folds and drove his tongue inside her, groaning as her wetness trickled into his mouth. Soon, Maude's low scream echoed in the antechamber, her head falling back onto the desk as she writhed with the force of her release. But he didn't cease his play when she quieted, he entered her sheath with two fingers and lazily fucked her with them until she moaned his name and implored him to fill her.

Yet still he denied himself, wanting to hear Maude spend again. Sliding his slick fingers further down, he penetrated her back entrance and pressed deep while he fluttered his tongue against her pearl. Maude's back arched, her wild cry the sweetest music to his ears as she found release once more. It was fortunate the stone walls of the castle were so thick, otherwise everyone in the village would come running. But as heavenly as it was to pleasure and prepare her, his rigid cock desperately needed relief. Not to mention that his leg would soon start aching unbearably if he kept all his weight upon it.

Rising to his full height, Keir grasped Maude's hips and tugged her forward so her backside rested at the edge of the desk. "I'm going to fuck ye. Has it been a while since you've had cock?"

"Y-yes," she whispered. "But it's different now. I want it. I'm ready for you."

"I'd not hurt ye for the world. So, I'll go slowly to start. But after that...hard and deep."

Wrenching at the ties securing his hose, Keir freed his throbbing cock and wrapped one hand around it, rubbing up and down the engorged length. Already pearly moisture gathered at the plum-colored head; he would not last long once he finally got inside her. With a rough groan, he swirled the tip of his cock in her juices, gliding it against the petal-soft folds until she sobbed.

"No teasing," she said, her cheeks flushed, her violet eyes glowing like the finest amethysts. "I need all of you."

Surely Maude knew she had all of him? That she was under his care and protection now? That back in the library when he'd said *me and mine*, he'd meant her as well as Sorcha?

Or perhaps she was just a pleasure-starved woman who'd had a terrible fright and wanted the release of a mindless fuck.

"Tell me who ye belong to," he demanded, raw in his sudden uncertainty. "Who ye think of. Who ye crave."

Maude's eyes flared wide and more moisture soaked his cock. "You," she breathed, circling her hips, trying to lure him inside her. "I belong to you. I think of you. I crave *you*. Please, Keir. I've been empty for so long. Fill me."

A primitive growl escaped his throat at her sweet submission. Guiding his cock to her entrance, he slowly began to push it inside her, inch by inch.

God's blood.

He'd known she was tight, that her sheath would pulse and clench around his length like a vise. He'd felt that with his fingers. But the sensation of her velvety walls closing around him, the wet heat bathing his cock, was indescribable. Nothing in the world could compare.

Maude moaned as he sank deeper and deeper, her head thrashing a little on the desk. But with her thighs spread wide and knees held at her chest, her greedy cunt sucking him in, all she could do was receive everything he had to give.

"How is that, angel?" asked Keir, when he was completely lodged inside her. Sweat bathed his forehead at the strain of holding back his release; not even his most fervent imaginings had prepared him for the wonder of being wholly joined with Maude at last.

"I'm full. So full," she replied unsteadily, her fingers gripping her knees so firmly they left imprints on her skin. "It aches. I cannot take anymore. But I want it. I want it so badly. To be fucked by you, a gifted lover who cares for my comfort and pleasure."

His control threadbare at this point, Keir tapped her knee. "Wrap your legs around my waist. Aye, just like that. Now, hold on."

He pulled back then rammed forward, so deep that it would surely be too much for her to bear. But Maude's heels near-gouged his arse, her fingernails shredding his shirt as she gripped his shoulders, one word hovering in the air as she made her desire plain with a gasping chant of *more*.

Mindless in his lust, his relief she was safe after their ordeal on the mountain, the joy of hearing such words as 'I belong to you, I think of you, I crave you,' out loud, Keir fucked her brutally hard, his rhythm both powerful and relentless in the game of advance and retreat. But as he'd feared, his balls swiftly tightened, and with a low roar he buried himself in her welcoming heat, releasing his seed in several violent, agonizingly pleasurable bursts.

Keir slumped forward, his thighs braced hard against the desk the only thing keeping him upright as he struggled to regain his wits. "Forgive me, angel. I was too eager."

Maude's soft lips grazed his cheek. "You're not seeking forgiveness because I only had two star-bursting, toe-curling releases, are you? That would be so very foolish."

"I wanted more pleasure for ye," he grumbled.

"Well then," she replied saucily, as her hand patted his bare arse. "I suppose we'll have to try again."

Keir grinned at the bawdy, possessive gesture. "Suppose we will."

It was the strangest, most beautiful thing to laugh and jest with a man when his cock was deep inside her. After so many years of pain and temper, of willing her mind a thousand miles away as her husband took his pleasure and gave none in return, to feel so safe with Keir, so wild and free and wanton, was nothing short of a miracle.

Maude patted his firm arse once more, just because she could. "I have a humble suggestion, though. That we adjourn to a softer surface?"

Keir grunted. "My legs and lower back would appreciate that."

She laughed. "As would mine. Oak is excellent for strength but unforgiving for a soon-to-be grandmother."

"Why do ye keep saying that, about being a grandmother soon? I ken how old ye are. How old I am. It is daft to think grandbabes or silver in your hair or lines on your skin would dull my need for ye. *Daft*."

Stunned, Maude rested her forehead on his shoulder. What she'd thought to be lighthearted banter, Keir had taken as her wielding her age like a longsword to test him, and he was probably correct. She had been testing him, so yearning for comfort and pleasure, so afraid of being treated badly again, that to protect herself she'd hurled what she believed to be a great flaw in his face. It was just so...*unusual* to be wanted for something other than her womb or healer's hands.

"You desire *me*," she said slowly. "Not as a tool for heirs or gain...just me, in your bed."

"Glad that's now clear in your learned mind," Keir replied irritably.

Maude smiled and nuzzled the crisp hair on his chest. Never had grumbling been so endearing. "I just required enough pleasuring to be sure."

"Ha," he said, easing his spent cock from her sheath. A wash of seed gushed in his wake. "Ye spoke of a softer surface?"

"The chaise over there by the wall is very comfortable. I often take a short restorative nap if I'm working on a new tonic or waiting for the ink to dry on recipes or patient notes...Keir!"

"What?" he said, his brow furrowing.

"Your leg is bleeding through the bandage! Sit down at once so I can apply more salve and redress it," Maude scolded, shuffling off the desk and attempting to haul him like a contrary bull over to the chaise. All the while knowing it was much harder to appear the stern healer who must be obeyed when she was naked, walking bow-legged after being fucked senseless, and had seed trickling down her inner thighs.

His hazel eyes glinted. "Sounds like ye wish another bargain, angel. What will tempt me to do your bidding?"

"A healed leg?" she replied tartly, but her lips twitched. The way he'd taken to calling her *angel* warmed her heart, even if he called every woman that.

"Surely ye can do better."

Maude rolled her eyes. "Very well. If you are a good patient and sit *meek as a wee lamb* as you once promised, there may be a reward after I tend that leg."

"What kind of reward?"

"The kind that involves my mouth and your cock."

Keir immediately limped over to the chaise to sit down. "A verra powerful argument. But don't be covering that beautiful body while you're poking and prodding, though. Seeing ye naked is part of my reward."

She snorted. "And when do I get to see you naked? It's hardly fair that you have shirt and hose on while I wear nary a stitch."

"Right now," he replied, grasping the hem of his linen shirt and pulling it over his head, before tossing it over to the pile of her ruined clothing. Then he removed his hose, although blessedly, he actually demonstrated caution in easing the fabric over his bandage rather than tearing the knee-length garment off.

Maude permitted herself one long look at his broad shoulders, hairy chest and flat stomach, those powerful legs...and his cock, currently partially hard and resting on his thigh. Such a fine figure, and the touches of silver in his long black hair only made him more attractive. No green lad, but a man of experience equally skilled in rubbing shoulders and kissing cunt. However, she couldn't spend all day licking her lips over him, not when this wound needed tending from the exertions of crawling through an underground tunnel to escape the fire, galloping on horseback here to the castle, then fucking her atop a desk.

After fetching her herbal satchel and a cushion to kneel on, Maude returned to his side and began unwrapping the linen bandage to examine his cut. The wound was oozing, but thankfully only blood. No doubt he'd bumped and scraped and reopened it burrowing along the tunnel to secure their freedom. For caution's sake, she would soak the cut with another robust dose of yarrow infusion, then more coneflower salve, before applying a fresh bandage. She didn't know exactly why, but wounds seemed to heal better when bandages were regularly changed. Possibly because nothing had time to truly fester underneath.

"I am still confident this cut will fully heal," she said at last.

"Good to hear. Will ye once again paint my leg purple like some monster from the depths of Loch Etive?"

"Yes. You'll be a purple loch monster and you'll love it."

Maude cleaned the wound and surrounding flesh with the

yarrow infusion, before using a small soft sponge to slather Keir's leg with several layers of coneflower salve so it would be *very* purple. It was hard to concentrate though, kneeling naked on a cushion and decorated with seed, feeling his intense gaze on her as she wrapped a fresh bandage about his leg. His blatant admiration made her blush and squirm, and even with a fire going to warm the antechamber, her nipples were taut in the cooler air. Far more distracting though: the way her pearl throbbed between her legs as Keir began handling his cock, gripping it firmly and moving his fingers up and down.

She quivered, needing two attempts to secure the bandage knot. "What...what are you doing?"

"Getting ready for my reward. I've been a good patient, have I not?"

"Very good," she admitted.

"Seems like I'm not the only one who needs to spend again. If ye are a good lady and suck my cock well, perhaps I'll pleasure ye in return."

Maude squeezed her thighs together. "What must I do?"

"Come here."

Shuffling forward with the cushion, she knelt between his legs, her blood heating at the sight of his fully erect cock. "And now?"

"Take me in your mouth. But touch yourself as well. I want to watch ye stroke that swollen bud."

Greedy to taste him once again, Maude engulfed the head of his cock in her mouth and began to suck. He was hot and salty...earthy...yet there was another flavor as well, and she moaned at the knowledge that it was their essence combined. How very wicked.

Keir twisted her hair around his fist, tugging it lightly until she moaned again and reached down to caress her slick nether lips, to circle her sensitive pearl. It just felt so good, and she could feel that luscious pressure building, those tingles inside her ready to unleash.

Abruptly she was pulled away from his cock, and Maude made a sound of displeasure. "What? Why did I have to stop?"

His eyes glittered. "Straddle my lap. I want to see your tight cunt stretched wide as ye take my cock."

Maude trembled with need, bracing her hands on his shoulders as Keir fitted his thick length to her entrance. She tried to go slowly, her breath hissing at the sensation of being impaled, but she was simply too wet with his seed and her own arousal. In moments, he was all the way inside and she whimpered with the urge to move.

"Keir..." she begged. "*Please*."

He cupped her breasts, his strong fingers pinching her nipples until she cried out at the sparks of pleasure arrowing to her center. Next, he gripped her hips; forcing her up and down, languidly to start, then faster and faster.

"So tight," he groaned. "So hot. The way ye clench my cock...feels so damned good."

Maude ground herself against him as release beckoned, teasing her, tormenting her with something just out of reach. Then Keir thrust brutally hard, a snarl tearing from his throat as his seed gushed within. Her world splintered, and with a sobbing wail she spent, her fingernails raking his shoulders as fierce waves of pleasure overcame her.

All she could do was cling to him, boneless in the aftermath of their lusty joining. But when one of his hands started to rub her back and the other smoothed her hair, a single thought became clear as a mountain stream in her mind.

He might want her for bedding alone, but she was falling in love with Keir Wright.

Saints alive.

CHAPTER 6

The following dawn, several candles lit to help him see, Keir lay propped up in bed as he once again attempted to master the art of plaiting. Naturally, he would rather be practicing with Maude's hair than strips of linen, but if he had her close by, plaiting was not the skill he would be perfecting.

He needed to learn this for Sorcha.

Keir studied the large primrose blanket-covered lump at the end of his bed. A lump that was definitely snoring, not snuffling. The bairn had moved from the guest chamber chaise at some unholy hour of the morning, her blanket dragging against the stone floor and a colorful curse escaping her mouth when her toe caught on the edge of a rug. How he'd managed to continue feigning sleep and not succumb to laughter at rough warrior words from a little girl's lips, he would never know. But when Sorcha climbed up onto the bed like a foundling still not entirely certain of her welcome, wrapping herself in the blanket with only her face peeping out, his heart had clenched once again.

He would hunt down the remaining Campbells responsible for the weaving house raid and Burke and Fiona's deaths, even if it took years. But before that, he would have his bloody vengeance against the MacIntyre clan member or members who had chained the door and set fire to their dwellings, no matter what the laird might say. Although in fairness, the scholarly, even-tempered Lord of Glennoe had been clearly aggrieved at the attempt on his mother's life. The more volatile Lady Isla and Alastair had been downright furious.

Aye, in the past, he had failed his niece. Never again.

"What are ye doing, Uncle?"

Keir gasped as though utterly shocked. "A talking blanket on my bed? Or is it a large caterpillar in a cocoon?"

Sorcha giggled and poked her tongue out. "Of course not. It's *me*. Ye have old eyes."

"Alas, that is well true."

"What are ye doing with that linen? It looks all knotted."

"It is," he sighed. "I'm practicing my plaiting so your hair doesnae look like a worm swived a dungeon rat."

"What is *swived*?"

"Errr, I just meant...I'm practicing so your hair won't look messy."

Sorcha sat up on her knees, her gaze unusually solemn. "I willnae mind, Uncle, if my hair is messy. If ye can plait it, that would be nice. I could do yours. Well, comb it at least. If ye want."

Keir rubbed his jaw as his eyes stung. "Suppose ye could," he replied gruffly. "But get dressed first. The waiting woman laundered your tunic and stockings. And wash your face, or Lady Maude will be displeased."

She groaned, shrugging off her blanket, sliding onto the floor, and stomping over to the neatly folded pile of clean garments like a player on a stage. But eventually she returned, dressed, her face washed, and holding a wooden comb that

Lady Isla had thoughtfully provided. "I'll comb your hair now. Then tie it with my lucky ribbon so it willnae hang down and cover your eyes while ye search for the unseelie who burned my home."

Any protest at her using a bright yellow hair ribbon rather than a scrap of leather or thin cord to secure his hair died on his lips. "I'm sure it will help. Always good to have a lucky hair ribbon."

Keir carefully swung his legs over the side of the bed and sat up so Sorcha could begin combing his hair. The wooden prongs scraping his skull and catching on what seemed like a thousand knots made him wince; dungeons really were missing a trick in not using this as a torture method to extract confessions. However, the comb soon slid through his hair easily enough, and he sighed in relief as she gathered it together and painstakingly tied it with the ribbon at the nape of his neck.

"There," Sorcha announced, handing him a plain brown ribbon. "Now me."

He took a deep breath as she stood in front of him. Surely, he could do this. It was just combing and a *plait*. "Aye. Be still, now."

With the concentration of a captain about to charge into battle, Keir gently pulled the comb through the knots and burrs in her long red locks. Sorcha hissed and wriggled a few times when he attended to some particularly stubborn knots, but eventually her hair was ready for plaiting. After parting it into three even sections, he cross-cross-tugged over and over, just as Maude had shown him, until he reached the end. Then he tied it with the brown ribbon, rather proud that it almost resembled a plait. A lumpy, crooked, uneven plait, but a plait all the same.

Sorcha patted it, shuddered, then turned and gave him a brave smile. "It's...good."

He laughed as he stood, smoothed his shirt and hose, and reached for a plain black velvet doublet lent to him by Alastair. The garment was small on him, but he was too grateful for the extra warmth against the morning chill to complain. "That is far kinder than I deserve, bairn. Shall we walk to the castle chapel for mass?"

"I suppose," she replied, her nose wrinkling. "I havenae been to chapel for so long. God might not remember me."

"Of course, He will. God remembers all."

Sorcha nodded. "We should fetch Lady Maude."

"Ye like her?" Keir asked as they crossed the chamber to the door, almost holding his breath because the answer mattered so much. He craved a future with the lady in it.

"Aye. Lady Maude is good at toasting and plaiting and making tonics. Also, she has pretty hair and smells nice. Her eyes are *purple*. Like that salve she put on your leg. Is your leg feeling better?"

He halted and flexed his leg, pleasantly surprised when it offered no more than a mild twinge in response. Perhaps it was just great skill, or the fact she received guidance from above, but the purple loch monster salve was so wondrous it should be carried about in a royal litter complete with musical procession and poetry odes. "Much, much better."

"Good. Ye were in the apothecary a verra long time."

Heat flushed his cheeks. "Aye, well, the clan healer likes to be thorough in her treatment."

So, so perfectly thorough.

As Keir yanked open the chamber door, unsure if he could manage anymore innocently pointed bairn comments, he came face-to-face with the lady herself.

"Good morning to you both," said Maude, with a soft smile. "I wasn't sure if you remembered where to find the chapel, Keir."

He studied her. She looked so beautiful yet so untouchable

in her ruby-colored velvet gown, with its laced-on sleeves, embroidered bodice, and a jewel-studded girdle at her waist. A low hood with a short headdress partially covered her hair.

Unease lanced him. Yesterday had been beyond magnificent, but now she was the highborn lady once more. Would duty overrule all else as long as they remained within the ancient stone walls of Glennoe Castle? Lady Isla might have given her discreet approval for a bedding, but that certainly didn't stretch to anything more, and it would be far too much to hope the laird and Alastair might consider a lowborn, unlearned, formerly-banished warrior as a suitable match for their mother. How could he convince them all that he was the only correct choice as Maude's second husband?

"Good morning," Keir replied formally, inclining his head and offering his arm, glad he could at least recall a few courtly gestures. "I think I remember, but we would appreciate an escort."

Maude's brow furrowed a little, but she placed one hand on his sleeve, and held out her other hand for Sorcha to take. "Come along, sweetling. We don't want to be late."

The chapel was on the ground floor, and although Glennoe Castle wasn't overly large, compared to his mountain dwelling it was a palace. They seemed to walk along hallways and round corners and down circular staircases for a week, but at last they stood in front of the chapel's wooden double doors. Even now he could smell incense and tallow candles, the familiar scent cloying as they entered the cool, darkened space. As usual, there were cushioned benches along two walls for the elderly, infirm, or pregnant; thankfully his much-improved leg meant he didn't need to join those seated.

It was odd being in a holy place after so long. He had much to be grateful for; Sorcha's good health, Maude's healing and soothsaying skills, them all escaping the fire, him at last having the opportunity to bed the woman he'd wanted for so long, even if he'd not declared the true depth of his feelings. But alongside that, he held such rage in his heart for so many injustices: the devastating losses of his brother and sister-in-law that weighed so heavily on his soul, and the blaze that had nearly cost him everything.

Keir clenched his jaw and crossed himself as Sorcha and Maude did the same. If he prevailed and found the clan member responsible, he would have so much more to seek absolution for.

☙❦❧

As it reminded her so much of her unhappy younger years with the baron, the chapel was Maude's least favorite place in the castle.

Once they had thankfully departed the room, she inhaled deeply of the fresher air, grateful for the sense of freedom. To feel powerful heavenly love, priests and incense and lengthy sermons on morality in no way compared to kneeling naked at her chamber window, bathed in sunlight. After standing in the darkened chapel, surrounded by others who were impatient or downcast or regretful as they endured their early morning lecture, she always left with a heavy heart. Where was the light? The hope? The inspiration to march on when all seemed lost? If priests spent even half as much time preaching joy as they did sin and vice, perhaps people would listen.

Maude pretended to cough to hide a scowl unbecoming of the laird's mother. Many of those milling around already thought her a witch, there was no need to strengthen that belief with a tirade against the oppression and unhappiness caused by religious edicts.

Perhaps one of those milling had tried to kill her and Keir and Sorcha.

The thought chilled her, and Maude rubbed her arms, abruptly desperate to return to her apothecary. At least in there the world made sense, and it had been the setting for the greatest pleasure she'd ever known. But how did Keir feel about her in the cold light of day now that the fright of the fire, chained door, and crawling along underground tunnels had diminished? He'd looked at her so oddly when she'd arrived at his chamber to fetch him and Sorcha. Almost like she was a stranger.

Surely, after his reassurance, it wasn't too soon for him to tire of her? Or now that he'd bedded her, was she just another notch on his headboard?

"Lady Mother?"

Maude almost yelped at Callum's gentle touch to her wrist, so lost had she been in her troubling thoughts. "My son. Did you need something?"

He studied her; his gaze concerned. "You looked upset. Is something amiss, or is it the lingering effects of yesterday?"

"I am quite well," she replied, forcing a smile. "Just wondering if the fire-starter dared to worship this morning."

Callum's mouth thinned. "I wondered the same thing. I know it is a plan with many flaws, but I've decided to question everyone who attends breakfast and have my scribes take written statements. I want to look into each face and hear their words, weigh them against the claims of others. They will all know the gravity of the matter."

"We have to start somewhere," she replied, nodding. "Even if a confession is unlikely, we may gain information to light our path or remove certain people from the list of suspects. Apart from Isla and Alastair, would you personally vouch for anyone?"

Her son met her gaze, his gray eyes sad. "My two scribes,

for they have been working long hours gathering old clan records into one tome. But as for the others...no. The fire-starter could be a guard, fishwife, shepherd, weaver, a cook... anyone."

Maude winced. "Keir and I both have our naysayers, which doesn't help."

"My lady?" said a deep voice behind her, and she turned so quickly to face Keir that she nearly stumbled.

"The laird has a plan," she whispered, before adding loudly, "I'm ready for breakfast. Sorcha, are you hungry? Shall we see what the kitchens provide us?"

The little girl, who continued clinging to Keir's hand, nodded cautiously. "Aye."

After Callum was joined by Alastair and Isla, the six of them walked to the great hall, also located on the ground floor but far away from the chapel. The large room was the favorite of many—spacious and airy, with several glass windows to welcome the light, and warmed by two fireplaces. Today it bore the delicious scent of freshly baked bread as servants brought out still-warm barley loaves with butter, boiled eggs, sliced venison from the previous night's supper, and jugs of small ale and watered wine.

The top table rested on a raised dais in front of the north wall. As laird, Callum always sat in the middle, Isla to his right and Alastair next to her. Maude moved to take her usual spot to Callum's left, but when Keir and Sorcha continued walking, clearly intending to sit at one of the trestle tables on the far side of the hall, Maude leaped forward and grabbed Keir's hand. "Will you both sit with me?"

He hesitated, his gaze on the other clan members who were filling the room. They all appeared eager for a good breakfast before they began their duties in the castle, outside tending the animals and fields, fishing in the loch, training with swords, or creating garments in the newly rebuilt weaving house. However, furtive looks and whispers were already starting at the presence of a banished warrior and his orphaned niece.

"I'm not sure that is a good idea," said Keir.

Maude almost groaned at her foolishness. He was quite correct. It would cause undue talk for him and Sorcha to sit at the top table. While the clan had eventually accepted that the laird and lady were part of a trio, they were young. The laird's widowed mother was supposed to sit in a corner like a potted plant and wither away in her grief. And yet...she wanted to keep Keir and Sorcha close by. Especially if the person who had committed such vile acts on the mountain was in this room, laughing and eating as though they didn't have a care in the world.

She bit her lip, unsure what to say next. Then Callum made the decision for her.

"Perhaps, Keir, you and Sorcha would do me the honor as special guests, to sit there at the end of that table closest to mine? I shall make an announcement to all present regarding the banishment, and address what happened on the mountain."

"As you command, laird," said Keir as he bowed, the relief and respect in his gaze both heartwarming and heart-twinging. While she welcomed his sincere deference to her son, it did sting a little that he didn't wish to start a scandal. Because it *would* be a scandal, a highborn English lady who was a companion of the king, choosing a formerly banished warrior without rank or heavy purse. One that would require all of her and Keir's mettle to prevail.

Argh. How much easier life would be if she was just a healer, free to love whom she pleased.

"Here you go, Sorcha," Maude said brightly, leading the girl over to the table Callum had gestured to. "Look, even a little velvet cushion on the chair. Grand as a princess. I'm sure your uncle will serve you some fine venison. Will you have small ale or watered wine?"

A feminine hand gripped hers. "Easy now, Mother," muttered Isla. "You are chirping like a baby bird. Come and sit. The servants will pour for Sorcha."

Maude's shoulders slumped as they walked arm in arm up onto the dais. "Forgive me. I'm hearing myself and yet I cannot stop."

"Keir has feelings for you, I'm sure of it. The way he watches you when you aren't looking...it is fiercely protective. But you must take this slowly in public. He's only just returned. Let the clan grow familiar with him again and understand that he is a good man, not at all the villainous knave your late husband claimed."

Her daughter-in-law was absolutely correct. Maude sighed, embarrassed at her display. "And, pray God, let us discover who is behind the crimes on Ben Cruachan."

Isla's gaze narrowed. "Oh, we will. And the punishment shall be harsh, even Callum is turning in that direction. Last night he was in such a state...I've never seen him thus, not even back at the tourney when he lost points in the sword-fights. Now, let us have breakfast. I am eating for two and refuse to wait any longer."

Once they'd taken their seats at the top table, servants trailed past with dishes of food to choose from. Maude selected some warm barley bread with butter, one boiled egg, and two slices of venison. However, each mouthful was a struggle, knowing what Callum was about to do. Would someone confess? Would they be able to tell truth from lies in an investigation? Chaining a door and setting a dwelling on fire with people inside was so evil, it was hard to imagine this was the first crime of those responsible. What if they'd done something terrible before?

Her stomach roiled at the thought; she pushed her plate

away and instead glanced down at Keir, who was carving venison for Sorcha. As though he felt her gaze, he looked up. And winked.

Maude let out a slow breath as some of her tension eased. The way he could comfort her without words was a rather wondrous gift.

Sitting back in her chair, she sipped some watered wine and observed the activity in the great hall. As usual, the sounds of so many people talking, eating, and drinking were near-deafening, but nearly all eyes were on Keir. Some clan members looked merely curious; others almost friendly. But far too many were viewing him with suspicion, or outright anger.

Callum needed to make his announcement. It was long past time Keir was accepted back into the clan, and not just for her sake. He had suffered far too much already.

࿐

Trapped in the dark abyss of his grief and guilt, the silence of the mountain and solitary meals in his sparsely furnished dwelling had been endlessly lonely. Yet here in this warm and noisy great hall, surrounded by more than a hundred others... Keir could feel the walls he'd built around himself cracking a little.

Already a few men from the village had offered hand-shakes or hearty claps to the shoulder, and they'd included him in their argument over ale or whisky being the finer drop. He'd been the target of several ribald jests as both a tavern wench and a weaver he'd spent evenings with in the past had bluntly asked if he wished to resume bedsport that evening. Those offers he'd politely declined.

But he'd missed this sense of belonging, even the stares and scrutiny and lack of secrets that went with life in a smaller clan. In Glennoe, the castle kitchens offered breakfast twice each week for all close by so the laird could make announcements, publicly approve betrothals, greet newborns, or share news of a death. Dispute trials were also heard in the great hall, but they were separate to the breakfasts and only held on the last day of each month. Unlike his father, Callum was a fair, generous and caring laird who put his people rather than war first.

He'd learned that from his mother.

Keir glanced over at Maude once again, unable to keep his gaze away for long. She was watching everyone eat, a pensive look on her face. Was she concerned about the investigation to come? What they might discover? That would be entirely understandable. It had certainly rocked him to the core knowing that someone from the clan had tried to kill her, him, and Sorcha. Perhaps someone he'd broken bread with, fought alongside, or bedded. But any friendship before yesterday wouldn't matter at all now. Not when they'd threatened what he held most dear.

"Uncle, I've eaten all my egg."

"Good lassie," he replied, nodding at Sorcha. "Do ye want something else, or is that belly full?"

"I hope it is full," said a laughing voice behind him, and he rose to bow at Lady Isla.

"How so?" he asked.

The Lady of Glennoe tilted her head in the laird's direction, then beamed. "I hoped to convince Sorcha to accompany me to the practice area for a lesson with a wooden sword. A lassie is never too young to learn a warrior's skills so she might protect the castle."

His niece gasped, her eyes bulging. *"A sword lesson?* Like how Uncle fights?"

"Indeed."

Sorcha's whole face lit up, but then she bit her lip and looked at him. "You might be sad without me."

Damned heart clench.

"Well, I'll miss ye of course," he said, very gruffly. "But imagine what you'll learn from Lady Isla, the finest sword-fighter in Scotland. I couldnae step in the way of that. Go on, now, be a good bairn, and I'll see ye soon."

Picking up a second piece of warm buttered barley bread, Sorcha gulped it down, grinning the entire time. Then she skipped away with her new tutor, firing questions like a hail of arrows, and Keir barely stifled a laugh. The laird's wife deserved the realm's highest honor for such a selfless act.

Moments later, a bell rang, and soon the great hall was remarkably silent.

Callum rose to his feet, his expression even. "Good morning, all. Before you go about your duties, I have some important announcements and I desire you to pass these words on to those who aren't here. First, you might have seen Master Keir Wright eating here today. He is a guest at my invitation."

A loud murmur started in the hall and the laird cleared his throat to silence it. "Keir's banishment is over. He is welcome, on my express orders, across MacIntyre land and to rejoin the clan guard should he so desire. I consider the matter that resulted in his banishment to be done and will neither accept nor condone any further punishment for it."

The murmurs were even louder this time, like a roll of thunder. Keir could practically feel countless eyes boring into his skull and it reminded him of his trial at the mercy of Donald the Bastard. This time, at least, he had a champion.

"I thank ye, my laird," said Keir, loud enough to be heard over the din.

Callum nodded and rang the bell a second time for quiet. "There is a second matter, a most grave one, that must be addressed. You may already be aware, but yesterday morning on Ben Cruachan, one or more people chained the door to Keir's dwelling and set it alight. Inside were Keir and young Sorcha Wright, but also my mother, who was attending Keir's badly cut leg. Thanks to Keir's skill and bravery, all three escaped without injury. However, his dwelling was burned to the ground, as was the one beside it belonging to his late brother and sister-in-law, Burke and Fiona Wright."

The laird paused deliberately as gasps echoed in the great hall. Keir glanced around, judging the expressions of those present, and to his relief, many looked genuinely horrified.

"Nae!" exclaimed one young man. "We've lived in peace since the raid."

"That would have been *murder*," added an older woman. "Was it the wretched Campbells again? The MacDonalds?"

"I don't believe so," said Callum, his voice sharpening. "Two words were painted on the outside wall of Keir's dwelling. Traitor and Witch. I have heard such terms in reference to Keir and my mother before; traitor for the fight between Keir and my late father, and witch against my mother's blessed gifts. Only someone in Clan MacIntyre could have known her exact whereabouts yesterday. The criminal or criminals responsible may well be in this room."

The great hall erupted in noise; shouts, even a few shrieks alongside tankards thumping and eating knives clattering onto the trestle tables as people loudly protested their innocence and denounced such heinous acts.

Keir leaned back in his chair, rubbing a hand across his jaw. Perhaps he should have ignored good sense and accepted Maude's tempting invitation to sit beside her at the top table. Then they could have bent their heads together and discussed the various reactions, if they were real or feigned, if someone appeared too relaxed or too nervous after the laird's pointed words.

But he sat down here, a world apart from Maude up on

the dais, and he didn't know her mind. He wanted to know it. To gain wise counsel or reassure her.

"What will ye do, laird?" called a young weaver from the back of the hall when the din eventually lessened a little.

Callum smiled, but there was a steely determination in his gray eyes. Aye, he was his mother's son, fortunately for the clan. "I shall conduct an investigation, starting today. I have scribes ready to take a sworn statement from each clan member as to their whereabouts yesterday morning, and the name of another two who can confirm that. Every dwelling shall be searched for pitch and brushes. There will be no exceptions for either, and no clan member will be granted leave from MacIntyre lands until this investigation is complete."

"Aye," added Alastair savagely, glaring at those in the hall. "If you have naught to hide, you have naught to fear."

After patting his lover's hand, Callum continued, "There will be two lines. Alastair and our lady mother will hear statements on this side of the room. Keir and myself will hear the rest on the other. No one may leave until they have spoken to us and reaffirmed their oath of loyalty; anyone who attempts to do so will cool their heels in the castle dungeon. As they have no stake in proceedings, I will dispatch my wife's Sutherland guards to begin the dwelling searches. Make no mistake...this is the gravest of matters and those responsible will be held fully accountable."

This time the reaction was far more muted; people talking in hushed whispers, their eyes wide, as kitchen servants tiptoed back into the great hall to remove the dishes and remaining food, and clean up any spills. Several guards then assisted in moving the trestle tables to clear a space for the two lines, and clan members arranged themselves in an orderly fashion, half in front of Alastair and Maude and the other half in front of a trestle table near the double doors.

A hand came to rest on Keir's shoulder. "If you'd care to join me, Keir?"

He turned and met Callum's gaze with his own. "I'd be honored, laird."

They walked together to the trestle table, two men cutting a swathe through the sea of people like a warship.

The laird leaned close as they sat down. "Do not fret about Sorcha outside, either. Isla is well-guarded and they will keep your niece safe. Like you, I do not risk me and mine. Especially now."

Keir nodded in gratitude. Knowing Sorcha was protected and well cared for eased his mind, now he could give all his attention to this upcoming task. They would hear a lot of stories and be able to ask questions if they desired, while scribes busily took notes with quill and ink.

One way or another they would find those responsible.

Then the guilty would pay.

Dearly.

CHAPTER 7

I t was amusing she'd thought the MacIntyres a smaller clan, because today she and Alastair had heard about seven thousand sworn statements.

Discreetly moving on her chair to ease her numb bottom and stretch her aching back, Maude waited for the next person to step up. Among the fervent denials of any wrong-doing and heartfelt pledges of loyalty to the laird and his family, there had been moments that made her smile. Like the rueful young lad rudely awoken by the pecking of impatient chickens when he'd overslept after a night embracing an ale barrel; he'd shown them the beak marks on his feet as proof. Or the scarlet-cheeked older couple who confessed they'd been inspired by the laird's happiness in a trio to invite their widowed neighbor over for supper, and all had stayed abed the next morning, even missing chapel.

The scribe had fumbled with his inkpot over that statement. Maude solemnly thanked them for their honesty, while Alastair just grinned and wished them well.

"Good morning, Lady Maude. Master Alastair."

She inclined her head at Colin MacIntyre, the clan blacksmith and a distant cousin of her late husband's. "Good morning, Colin. How do you fare?"

Surprisingly, the usually amiable man of about sixty summers looked very troubled, tapping one foot and hunching his well-muscled shoulders, strong from the toils of his craft. "I was distressed t'hear of the misfortune, lady. 'Tis glad I am that ye and Keir and the wee lassie came to nae harm. Because..."

Beside her, Alastair sat up straighter in his chair. "Because?"

Colin pursed his lips and leaned down. "Some items were stolen from my smithy. The lads have a table where they keep all the pieces for polishing before delivery. Yesterday morning...some were missing. We turned the smithy upside down to look for them, perhaps just misplaced, ye ken? But nae. And one of those items was the bigger steel fire striker I made for the castle kitchens so the servants wouldnae singe their fingers so much."

Maude went still as her neck prickled. "I know you are careful with your fine pieces, Colin. And that you chain your smithy doors at night so no one wanders in and hurts themselves with sharp tools or smoldering coals."

"Aye, madam. The door chains were gone too."

"How *interesting*," said Alastair in a low, deadly voice.

The blacksmith flinched. "My loyalty has ere been to Clan MacIntyre and I would never harm ye, Lady Maude, not when ye brought my good wife safely through five births. Nor would I hurt a wee bairn, or Keir. I have nae quarrel with him, he is a fine swordsman who never should have been banished for a bloody—er, begging ye pardon, lady—a punch."

"Why didn't you report this theft sooner?" asked Maude as calmly as she could when she wanted to shriek in frustration.

Colin hung his head. "I wanted tae be certain. We searched my dwelling, the garden, animal pens, even down by the loch shore. In the event it was a trick or jest gone too far that no one would admit tae. Some folk are daft with a belly full of ale and they dinnae remember what they've done. But it was theft for sure. I ask that my dispute be heard by the laird, for it seems someone stole a fire striker and chains from me to use for evil purpose."

Her stomach roiled, and Maude pressed her fingers to her lips so she didn't lose her breakfast. It was one thing to strongly suspect a clan member to be responsible for the heinous acts on the mountain, quite another to have that theory confirmed with further evidence. Never would she believe that Colin or his family were capable of such hateful crimes; the blacksmith was not only amiable to all, but scrupulously honest and hardworking. He'd never called her witch, either, not once in twenty-six years.

But someone had involved Colin in their terrible plan. Did they think the blacksmith would be blamed just because his tools were used?

Alastair cleared his throat. "Thank you for your time, Colin. I know you hate to be away from your smithy. I shall inform the laird about your dispute and it will be heard this month's end. If you'll just wait while the scribe reads back what he's written, then make your mark to agree the words are fair and true."

"Aye," said Colin as he listened intently to the scribe. Then he nodded, and scratched out his mark with the quill. "Fair and true. May God give ye good counsel and swift feet. We cannae have someone in our midst who would do murder."

After the blacksmith departed, Maude and Alastair exchanged a glance. Her foster son appeared ready to upend the trestle table, and she knew the effort he was exerting not to march over to Callum for a restorative kiss. In truth, she wanted to run to Keir for the same reason. But there were still several people standing in their line, and this task couldn't be delayed. Everyone had duties to get to and it was approaching mid-morning now.

Maude gulped some watered wine to fortify her nerves, then forced a smile on her face for the next two people, a young dairymaid and her fisherman husband. Neither had anything of note to add, and with a two-year-old child, it was hard to imagine the haggard-faced couple going up Ben Cruachan to commit crimes when they could be napping. Then came a face she'd seen recently: Ida MacTier. The elder stood next to her daughter-in-law Heather, who was carrying her tightly swaddled and thankfully sleeping newborn son. Ida was frowning darkly, Heather had reddened eyes and kept sniffling.

"Ida. Heather," said Alastair, quite gently for him. "Good morning."

"Aye Alastair, but it's nae good, nae good at all," said Ida sharply. "My heart won't stop pounding...tae think...our Craig and me just on the mountain with Sorcha, then that evil happens! Were we being watched even then? I give thanks to God those dwellings were all that Keir and Sorcha lost, although that is bad enough. The laird must strike a harsh blow when he finds out who did this. His own *mother* nearly killed."

Heather dabbed at her eyes. "I went to use the p-privy after feeding my babe...I saw the flames and smoke from d-down in the clearing. My scream woke up Mother and Craig... we ran to fetch buckets, then on the path we met the laird and all those guards. They took the buckets and told us to shelter inside. Oh, praise the saints ye are safe, lady, and Sorcha and Keir. How f-frightening it must have been."

Maude nodded, not sure she could endure much more

outpouring of raw feeling when her own emotions were so close to the surface. Now she needed far more than a restorative kiss from Keir; more like an endless hug and her hair stroked until this terrible heaviness lifted. No one else would do. Not ever. She was most certainly in love with Keir Wright, and once this nightmare had passed—which she could only pray would be soon—he and Sorcha would be sitting at the top table. Anyone else's opinion be damned. Even her beloved sons.

She *deserved* happiness.

"It was frightening," said Maude eventually. "And thank you. Is Gavin not here today?"

Heather shook her head. "It's his turn to guard the borderlands watchtower. But I'll ensure he comes here and makes a statement as soon as he returns, I swear."

"Aye," said Alastair, patting her hand. "I know you will. Is Craig well? Not upset?"

"He was much better after he heard Sorcha was unharmed. He's with our neighbor and her bairns now, so me and Ida could attend chapel. We take turns minding the young ones."

"Good. Then make your mark, and you can hurry home before that sweet-faced babe wakes up," said Maude, and the scribe helpfully began reading from his parchment.

Ida snorted, bending to sign her name. "Ye have the right of it, Lady Maude. He's a wee terror when hungry. Might crack the castle walls with his wails."

"Good healthy lungs, at least."

"Too healthy," muttered Heather as she added her mark. "Craig was the same. The boys bellow like their father."

After they'd waved the two women away, Maude and Alastair heard from one more man, a cowherd just returned from selling weaned calves at the Crieff cattle market. Like most others, he had nothing of interest to add.

When the great hall was empty at last and the scribes had trotted away, Maude slumped back in her chair. "Mercy."

Alastair helped her to her feet. "Come, Mother. Let us go meet privately with Callum and Keir; they need to know what Colin told us. Then you can flee to your apothecary. I'll check on Isla, but am quite certain neither she nor Sorcha will want to come inside just yet."

"I daresay," she agreed fondly as they stepped off the dais and walked toward the hall entrance where the other two men were talking quietly.

In some ways, it was pleasing that Callum's plan had procured at least one piece of useful information, but another part of her worried at what might lie ahead. If the culprit was determined, this might be just the beginning.

৩৮৩

"...and then Colin informed us that someone had stolen items from his smithy. A large steel fire striker that he made for the castle kitchens. And the chains that he uses to secure the doors so no one gets in and does foolish things with sharp tools and hot coals after they've had too much ale."

Keir clasped his hands together at Maude's words so he didn't pick up something breakable and hurl it against the library wall. His woman looked as exhausted as he felt after hearing statements from so many clan members; looking them hard in the eye, weighing their words against the words of others, making a judgement if they were being truthful or evasive. It appeared everyone had been honest with him and the laird, but none of them had provided something as useful as Colin's information. Something as shocking.

To have stolen chains and a fire striker meant the mountain attack was *planned*. Not done on a whim or a drunken mistake.

Someone had purposefully set out to kill him, Maude, and Sorcha.

"So," said Keir quietly. "Whoever did this *intended* murder."

Callum abruptly stood and marched over to a desk set with whisky decanter and several fancy drinking glasses. They appeared flimsy compared to pewter goblets or wooden tankards, but the laird seemed to like them. "Whisky anyone? Yes, I'm aware 'tis not yet noon."

"Aye," said Keir.

"A large one," said Alastair, drumming his fingers on the arm of the chaise.

"Even bigger for me," said Maude, twisting a lock of hair around one finger; the act of someone with far too much weighing on their mind.

The laird poured generous servings of whisky for everyone, then handed them around. For several minutes the library was eerily quiet as they each stared at the amber liquid before gulping it back. The whisky burned a little as it went down, but soon Keir's throat practically hummed as it was warmed with a peaty glow. It was far, far too long since he'd had a drink as fine as that; whisky was indeed the water of life.

"Now we're all fortified," said Keir. "What next?"

Callum ran a hand through his rumpled hair; further evidence of his disquiet. The laird was usually immaculately turned out. "I'll receive a report from the Sutherland guards about their search of each dwelling this evening. There are still some statements to be taken. But no one has confessed... or attempted to flee. This troubles me greatly."

Alastair nodded grimly. "They feel no guilt."

A thought struck Keir and the words leaped from his tongue. "Do ye think they've maybe done something heinous before, were not caught, so grew even bolder?"

"I wondered the same," said Maude softly. "And when I think of heinous acts...I think of the weaving house raid."

"A party of Campbells," said Callum, frowning. "We know that."

Keir stared at his hands. He did indeed know, for without clan duties he'd had time to stalk several of the enemy and deprive them of their innards. But something about that raid had never sat quite right with him: how easy it had been for the Campbells to attack in broad daylight. Like they'd known all the hidden paths and shelters on MacIntyre land.

Like they'd had assistance from someone who knew those paths and shelters.

However, he'd not witnessed the raid, only experienced the hideous aftermath when a castle messenger rode to inform him of the deaths. So he had no proof to support his musings. But now, after the fire...

"Just Campbells?" he asked. "Or perhaps Campbells with the help of a friendly MacIntyre?"

"Saints alive," said Maude, her face parchment pale.

"No," snapped Callum, getting to his feet once more and pacing the library. "Surely no one would betray the clan like that...damn it, I don't know. I'm not sure of anything anymore."

"Forgive me, laird," said Keir contritely. "I didnae mean to add to ye burdens. And I don't have any proof of a rat in the kitchen. I could be completely wrong."

"I'm not so sure you are," said Alastair. "But last year was fraught with impossible tasks for Callum. Repairing all the trade and friendship treaties the old laird fractured. Then that deadly raid, losing the weaving house, all those funerals, his cousin Red circling to take over...to save the MacIntyre clan we had no choice but to attend the tourney and win Isla's hand. After that we had to rebuild before Christmastide and winter set in. If there was a rat, he or she has had ample time to allay any suspicion and plot further evil deeds."

God's blood.

Leaning forward, Keir rested his elbows on his knees and reached down to adjust his leg bandage, just to clear his head of the churning emotions pounding against his temples. Not for the world would he trade places with the laird and his thousand cares...but if someone...anyone...in the village had voiced a concern, would he have investigated and perhaps halted a madman?

"Keir?" asked Callum swiftly. "Are you well? Forgive me, I have asked too much of you after your injury."

Before he could answer, Maude rose to her feet. "My patient must rest while I examine his leg for seepage or festering. As you all well know with cuts, this needs to be done each day. He is also due for another dose of white willow bark tea. Let us go now to the apothecary, Keir."

In other circumstances, he might have protested that his leg currently suffered no discomfort, but he was too grateful to Maude for sensing his urge to leave. Although in fairness, it appeared she needed to catch her breath as much as he did, and neither wished to worry the laird further.

"As ye say, healer," Keir replied, nodding respectfully as he also stood, deliberately swaying a little to add truth to her excuse. "Let me know, laird, if ye require me for anything else. I appreciate your words to the clan in the great hall."

"I meant them," said Callum. "We can make ready your old cottage in the village, or perhaps one of the unused dwellings in the castle grounds. And I know the less experienced guards, and my wife while she is with child, would greatly value a swordsman of your skill returning to the fold."

Keir inclined his head, not entirely sure if the laird would be so generous if he knew what had occurred between his lady mother and a lowborn guard. But that was a conversation for another day. "I shall consult with Sorcha, as she'll be living with me. But I'm sure now she's had a taste of sword lessons, she'll want more and to be close to the castle."

Maude smiled briefly. "I've no doubt of that. Now, come along, Keir. I must see to that leg."

They walked in silence to her chamber, her hand resting on his sleeve, and the warmth of her skin felt like a brand on his. Yet the moment they were alone in the cozy and heavily-scented apothecary, Maude made a sound of frustration and tore away her hood and headdress before throwing them onto the chaise.

"Talk to me," said Keir. "I know there is much weighing on your mind."

She shuddered and returned to him, resting her cheek against his chest. The simple act of such trusting affection brought every single protective instinct he possessed to roaring life. He wrapped his arms around her, holding her tightly against him, and brushed a kiss across the top of her head.

"I cannot even think right now," whispered Maude, as her trembling hands delved under his shirt to press against his back. "After Colin's words about the thefts from his smithy... and your thoughts on a rat in the kitchens...this is my fault. I did not foresee the raid. I could not save Burke or Fiona or the others from their injuries. I led the clan for an entire week while my sons were at the tourney and did not think to investigate further. I failed you. I failed Sorcha. And it is tearing me apart."

"Nae," he replied fiercely, stroking her silky hair. "'Tis not your fault. Dinnae let the darkness in others dim your light to serve or stop those gifts that bring joy and comfort. But more than that...do ye know how precious ye are to me? Ye are *mine*."

Maude leaned back, tilting her face up to him, her violet eyes huge. "Am I truly?"

"Aye."

"Then show me," she demanded, moving her hands to his chest and running her fingertips through the hair there, even tugging it a little.

Losing all control, Keir gripped the back of her neck to hold her still for his mouth, then swooped down with bruising force to capture her lips with his. She tasted like whisky and he groaned, kissing her, twining his tongue with hers as though this was their last day together. Maude whimpered and tried to pull him closer, her fingernails scoring his flesh as she rubbed herself against him, but her heavy velvet gown with its train was getting in the way and she mewled in distress.

"Easy, angel," he said thickly, gripping a handful of velvet so he could lift it up and free her legs. "Your man will take care o' ye."

As a good lover should.

৬♨৩

It didn't feel like they'd come together in this room with such ferocious passion just yesterday. That surely was a hundred years ago, and her body thirsted for Keir as a barren landscape thirsted for rain. Much like the first rays of dawn on her bare skin, Keir's touch gave her strength.

Maude burrowed against him. "Hurry. Please, please hurry."

He curled an arm around her waist, lifting her off her feet and walking her backward to the antechamber door. Then he braced her against it.

Oh. There could be no escape with sturdy oak behind and a man-mountain in front, and knowing she was at Keir's mercy, knowing all she could do was wrap her thighs around his hips and her arms about his neck, caused wetness to trickle from her aching center. When he reached between them, delving under her gown to part her bush and stroke her slick flesh with a blunt fingertip, she moaned.

Keir grunted. "You'll not get my cock yet, angel. Not until my fingers are drenched and I can lick them clean."

Maude cried out in protest, desperate to be filled, but the stubborn man merely teased her pearl, circling and circling the swollen, sensitive bud until she writhed against the door in an agony of need. At last he granted her a boon, sliding two fingers inside her soaked sheath and fucking her with them, but his actions weren't nearly fast enough or deep enough to compel the release she craved.

"*Keir*," she said, his name a plea.

He nuzzled her neck, the gentle affection a diabolical torment when her body screamed for rough and raw. "The way ye say my name when ye need to spend...it makes me so hard."

Wicked man, making her wait!

Maude slapped his shoulder, arching her mound against him in a futile effort to get his fingers deeper. "If you don't fuck me this minute, Keir Wright...I'll...I'll..."

"You'll what, angel?"

"Find another lover!" she lied blatantly, for who could possibly compare to a gruff Highlander who pleasured and protected in equal measure?

Keir's gaze narrowed. "Beg pardon?"

"You heard me."

"I thought I made it quite clear before," he said slowly, withdrawing his hand from between her legs and licking his fingers clean of her honey. "Ye are mine."

"In your head, perhaps. But I am English and you're Scottish so there are bound to be language misunderstandings. If you *showed* me though..."

His lips twitched. "Such a saucy wench, Lady Maude MacIntyre."

"Yet also correct."

"Aye," he said, tugging at the laces of his hose to free his hard cock. "Now ask me nicely, and ye may get what ye crave."

Maude quivered as he lazily teased her entrance with the engorged head. It felt enormous, but she couldn't wait any longer to have his full length inside her. "Please may I have your cock?"

"Where, angel? Tell me exactly where ye need it. Otherwise, we may suffer...now, what did ye call it? A language misunderstanding?"

Vexing, canny Scot, using her teasing against her.

She blushed. "Please may I have your cock in my *cunt*. Was that plain enough for—oh!"

The brutal thrust of his shaft robbed her of breath; her inner walls both protesting the stretch and eagerly welcoming the thick fullness that caressed every inch and brought her to pulsing, tingling life. When he immediately withdrew, she made a sound of dismay, but equally quickly he was lodged inside her once more, the start of a steady, heady rhythm that had her moaning in rapture.

"Oh, ye like that?" he asked, doing something with his hips that rubbed his groin directly against her aching pearl. She nearly swooned at the resulting burst of sensation.

"Again, Keir," Maude said breathlessly, digging her heels into the backs of his thighs, so close to release she could scarcely think. "Again and again."

The second time he did it, her core clenched around his cock and she screamed into his shoulder, at last reaching that glorious, shattering peak that hurled her into sweet bliss. Two thrusts later he followed her over the edge, a low roar echoing in the antechamber as his seed gushed inside her.

"I dinnae ken how," gasped Keir, his forehead resting against hers. "But it keeps getting better."

"I know," she whispered, trailing her fingers through his hair and lightly scratching the back of his neck, content to never move again.

A knock sounded somewhere near her head. Maude stared at Keir in the befuddlement of post-release mind fog, before understanding dawned. Each attempted to move away from the door and right their clothing. Naturally, all that happened was two sets of exhausted limbs buckled, sending them both into a laughing, groaning heap on the thankfully soft woven rug.

"Cramp," said Keir, clutching his foot. "Toe cramp!"

"P-press it to the f-floor and stretch it," said Maude, giggling helplessly as she hitched up her gown and attempted to knee-walk over to a nearby pitcher of well water, all while cupping her mound so she didn't trail seed across the floor. Pleasure and laughter in the midst of dark days? Keir Wright was indeed a heavenly gift.

As she snatched up a damp cloth and attended to the mess, the knock came again, more frantic this time. Swallowing several choice words, Maude put the cloth back down and walked bow-legged to the antechamber door, trying to compose herself. Alas, the sight of Keir cursing as he hopped over to the chaise, holding his cock, one shoe off, and hose gaping to reveal his bare backside, provoked more giggles.

"Dinnae laugh, woman, my hopping was more impressive than your waddle. And me with a toe twitching like a landed trout as well," he scolded, as he carefully tucked his cock back under his hose and fastened the ties.

"Forgive me," she choked out merrily, pausing briefly to smooth her hair. Nothing at all could be done about her crumpled gown. *That* she would have to shamelessly lie about. Then she pulled open the door. "Yes?"

A waiting woman stood there, wringing her hands. "Oh, my lady...beg pardon for disturbing ye when you're with a patient, but the castle is in an uproar—"

Maude's heart plummeted like a rock into the ocean. What now? Sorcha was safe with Isla, Callum and Alastair were in the library, and all the guards were at their posts.

"An uproar?" she asked sharply. "Why?"

"We just received word from the border...the king himself approaches!"

Maude stared, slack-jawed. He'd not said anything in his letter about a visit! "James?"

"Aye! Of course, our Jamie, who else?" the woman replied impatiently. "On horseback with ten men, no official party or carts following, so a secret visit. And he'll wish to see his good friend at once, I'm sure."

She ground her teeth against the sly implication they were far more than friends. Just because James's charm and bedchamber prowess was renowned the length and breadth of Scotland, did not mean he'd lifted her gown. The truth was, she'd once done the king a great service and he'd declared himself in her debt. They had corresponded for many years; the debt finally repaid when he'd discreetly aided Callum and Alastair at the royal tourney—by ignoring Isla's stealthy visits to help Callum improve his sword fighting, and making favorable pronouncements to ensure he reached the final four.

James was a good man; she loved him in a brotherly fashion. Unfortunately, he'd arrived at the worst possible time. What if the person responsible for the fires struck again while the king was here? Clan MacIntyre wouldn't survive.

"Lay out a fresh gown for me, please," said Maude briskly, her mind whirling at the possible disasters and consequences. "This one is...er, in need of laundering. I spilled white willow bark tea on it. Oh, and send someone to the weaving house to fetch a new shirt and hose for Keir Wright, and a tunic and shift for Sorcha Wright. This will be a good opportunity to show His Grace the clan's great skill."

"Aye, Lady Maude."

The waiting woman bobbed a curtsy, then departed.

Maude cleared her throat, and turned to Keir. "The king is coming, of all things. James is not a difficult guest, but after what has transpired, his visit could not fall upon a worse day."

"I heard," he replied, his gaze revealing nothing. "Dinnae fret, though, I'll not say anything about us in his presence."

Her heart sank. Not him too! "Keir—"

"Thank ye for arranging fresh clothing for myself and Sorcha; I'd best return to my chamber to wait for it. I hope the laird and Alastair have something soothing for poor Lady Isla after the thousand questions she's probably had to answer."

As Keir walked toward the door, he did halt to press a brief kiss to her cheek, but it was nowhere near what she wanted after their heated coupling. Bah. Why did James have to arrive today when everyone was so unsettled and a would-be murderer still roamed?

It was hard to imagine this visit being anything other than perilous.

CHAPTER 8

How did a swordsman compete with a king?

Keir scowled from his uncomfortable position on one knee as their sovereign pulled up his stallion in the castle courtyard, dismounted like he'd ridden for a half hour rather than days, and proceeded to charm everyone within a mile of where he stood.

A better question might be: how did an irritable old warhorse like Keir Wright, a man with naught but the clothes on his back and a single sword, compete with the young, handsome, learned, wealthy, exceedingly well-dressed James IV of Scotland?

Far worse than all those virtues, though, the king was so wretchedly *amiable*. And possessing a will of iron; it took a great deal of strength to take a realm broken after his father's disastrous reign, and slowly, painstakingly, join it back together. James had quelled rebellions and won battles. Built the jaw-dropping Great Hall at Stirling Castle, the largest in Scotland and renowned for its limewashed golden glow. He'd even wed a child he didn't love in the form of Margaret Tudor so there might be peace with England.

If Keir didn't want to snap the king in half for his closeness to Maude, he might have liked him very much. But that was impossible, especially as James currently walked arm in arm with Maude while the laird, Lady Isla, and Alastair introduced him to prominent members of the clan. And they were all coming this way. Sorcha was nearly beside herself; he'd already had to tug her back down onto one knee *twice* so she didn't fling herself at the reigning monarch and question him about crowns. Or princesses. Or what his horse liked to eat.

"Your Grace," said Callum eventually. "May I present Master Keir Wright and his niece Sorcha, special guests at the castle while they decide on their future."

The king inclined his head, dusty but resplendent in a blue velvet doublet with pearl buttons, finely embroidered shirt, dark hose, short cloak lined with ermine, and polished boots. He wasn't much taller than Maude, barely reaching Keir's collarbone, and possessed neatly kept, shoulder-length brown hair, fine features, and a clean-shaven jaw. Yet there was a warmth to James's smile and a twinkle in his eye that promised a merry time with those he considered friends.

"Master Wright," said the king in Gaelic, holding out one bejeweled hand for Keir to kiss. "We've not met before; I am glad to remedy that today. I was grieved to hear of your losses, but am pleased that Glennoe lifted your banishment, for that broken nose was undoubtedly well deserved. I'm sure you will fare much better with the new laird. He is worthy of the title."

Keir slowly rose to his feet, wincing a little as his fatigued limbs protested the movement. "Aye, Your Grace. The clan is most fortunate."

"Is your injury troubling you?"

"Nae. Sometimes I forget I am forty-five summers when engaged in...certain vigorous activities."

Maude's cheeks went pink, but she said nothing.

The king barked out a laugh and clapped Keir's shoulder. "A man is only as old as he feels, except when his knees remind him. Now, this bonnie bairn beside you is young Sorcha?"

Sorcha peered up at James while clinging tightly to Keir's hand. "Are ye really the king?"

"I am indeed," said James, crouching down so they were face to face. "And you're a brave, brave lassie fetching help for your uncle and crawling through tunnels."

Sorcha nodded. "Lady Isla showed me how to hold a wooden sword today. I am going to learn fighting like Uncle Keir, then kill the unseelie who burned our dwellings on the mountain."

"I see," replied the king gravely, before removing a small gold brooch from his short cloak and placing it in her palm. "Take this. It will help with your noble quest. And pay close heed to Lady Isla, for she can teach you much in a short time. Is that not so, Glennoe?"

"A perfect truth, Your Grace," said the laird, smiling at both his wife and Alastair.

"Then shall we retire inside? If you can forgive the dusty state of me, I am looking forward to some good Western Highlands hospitality," said James as he grinned and winked at Maude.

Keir almost hissed. Just when he'd began to thaw toward the king for being so kind to Sorcha and presenting her with a costly brooch, he had to go and say that. *Hospitality*. Ha. Everyone in Scotland knew what that meant; fathers, brothers, and husbands across the realm had been turning the other cheek for years to receive favor and gifts. Even more so on the birth of a babe. How many illegitimate bairns did James have now? Five?

Donald bragging about his wife bedding the king had

been bad enough. But seeing James act so familiar with Maude was enough to make him spit nails.

"Uncle! Hurry up. Everyone is going inside."

He glanced down at Sorcha who was valiantly trying to tug him toward the castle steps. With a clean face, brushed hair, new dark green tunic with thistles embroidered on the hem, and now the gold brooch, she looked like a little princess herself. "Aye, your highness."

As it was late in the afternoon, the final meal of the day was about to be served. However, with the king's unexpected arrival, the meal would now be a banquet complete with entertainment, and Keir was curious to see what they'd been able to manage. Maude claimed the king wasn't a difficult guest, but he was still the king, and no household or castle wanted to be known for a lackluster table. The shame would last years. Perhaps generations. Scots held long memories like that.

Forcibly quelling his irritation, Keir escorted Sorcha to the great hall. Once again Callum had generously seated them in a position of honor near the top table, but seeing Maude directly next to James, watching him pour her a goblet of wine and whisper in her ear, made his blood boil. Why couldn't kings just keep to their array of princesses and duchesses and queens and leave the other women be? Maude had enough to contend with. They all did, really. What if the criminal they searched for was here right now, sipping wine?

"Uncle Keir, ye are growling. Like an angry dog."

"Hush and have some sweetmeats," he replied as they sat in their cushioned chairs. "Not too many, though, or you'll get a bellyache."

About a quarter hour later, servants started bringing out dishes from the kitchens. Usually, an occasion like this would commence with some sort of subtlety, a sugar sculpture served before each course. However, with so little preparation time before word of the king arrived, this was politely ignored. But other delicious scents filled the hall—freshly baked barley and rye bread, also the heavy brown bread that served as trenchers. There was also roasted venison and chicken, fresh fish with a lemon sauce, and a thick beef stew with vegetables. More dishes would come out with the second course.

Keir draped Sorcha's napkin over her left shoulder, then attended to his own. He would eat carefully at this banquet; the embroidered linen shirt, hose, and dark brown velvet doublet provided by the weaving house were the finest garments he'd ever worn. And, miracle upon miracle, they actually fit him. He might be inferior to the king in every way, but at least he wasn't dressed like an old warhorse. Clan MacIntyre was highly regarded for their weaving and traded great quantities of hose and garters across the Highlands; another reason why the deadly Campbell raid had cut so deeply.

Sorcha tapped her spoon and eating dagger on the wooden trestle table. "Uncle, I would like, ummmm...fish. No, chicken. And beef stew, but ye can eat all the vegetables."

"Eat your own vegetables. How will ye lift a sword otherwise?"

She nodded reluctantly. "Maybe a few, then. But not turnips. I dinnae like turnips."

Keir grunted. "Turnips should be used for naught but testing the sharpness of a blade."

They exchanged a glance of complete accord and that damned heart clench sneaked up on him once more. But then the king rose to his feet, rang the laird's silver bell, and everyone in the hall fell silent.

"Friends," said James, bestowing a regal smile on all present. "I know my arrival was unexpected, but it is my honor to sup with you this day. I offer my gratitude to the esteemed Lord of Glennoe, his fair Lady Isla, companion Alastair, and my beloved friend Lady Maude, for their warm welcome. It has long been my wish to visit this castle, and I know we will have a merry time. God bless and keep you all. Cruachan!"

A rousing cheer went up at the MacIntyre battle cry, and Keir stifled an oath. Yet another of the king's skills, the gift of oratory.

But he would not just concede defeat like those other fathers and brothers and husbands. Maude belonged to him. He would not give her up without a fight.

"Have I told you how beautiful you look in that silver gown, Lady Maude? Like a star fell down from the heavens to sit among mere mortals."

Maude gritted her teeth at the king's extravagant compliment as she spooned up another few mouthfuls of tender roasted chicken from her trencher. It was true, the satin gown embroidered with silver thread did look lovely against her white-blond hair and violet eyes, much more than most colors. And she adored the way it sparkled in the flickering light of the great hall's beeswax candles. But she couldn't concentrate on foolish fancies this evening, not when someone intent on murder still lurked in their midst. The only reason she ate at all was the knowledge that the king's taster had sampled each dish before it was served to their table.

Someone who chained doors and set fires was capable of anything, including poison.

"Thank you," she said politely. "You also look well in your blue velvet and ermine trim...if a little weary."

James's eyes widened. "That might be an accurate observation, but no sugar to sweeten it from my favorite English-woman? One royal heart, crushed to powder in an instant."

"Surely your wife is your favorite Englishwoman."

"Do not even jest, my dove. Margaret is a child in my eyes, and with her high-and-mighty Tudor ways...it is more difficult keeping her happy, and thus old Henry happy, than I ever imagined."

Maude sighed and patted his hand. Then she leaned closer to not be overheard. "A duty marriage is a terrible burden, especially when you have all the trappings of it and not yet the required heir. But I greatly admire you leaving the queen be until she is older and better able to carry a child. When I think of how her grandmother must have suffered..."

The king grimaced. "Why do you understand when so many others do not? I have courtiers, nobles, and clergymen in my ear every day about a prince in the cradle, but I cannot lie with her. Not yet. And these same people scold me for finding pleasure elsewhere, running with tales to England about how I insult their princess. At least I have your letters, which bring me some comfort."

"I think you have far more in your life than my letters bringing you *comfort*, Your Grace."

"Maybe one or two things," he replied, a grin lifting his lips once more as he curled his fingers around hers. "Although I will be forever grateful I met you. Who would have thought such a terrible beginning could result in such a lasting trea-sure for me?"

Unable to help herself, Maude smiled in return. The king had always been charming, and it never surprised her that women up and down the realm fell eagerly into his bed. But she preferred a different side of him: the serious scholar. James was very intelligent with an excellent memory for detail; he spoke eight or nine languages with great fluency including Gaelic, and possessed an unquenchable thirst for the new and undiscovered.

They had met in dire circumstances. On his first visit to the Western Highlands nearly twelve years prior, James had sailed with several important nobles and courtiers to Dunstaffrage Castle at the mouth of Loch Etive to hear pledges of loyalty from local clan chiefs...and they'd all promptly been felled by dysentery. As she already had a reputation for skilled healing, an urgent message arrived at Glennoe Castle, and she'd ridden back with the guards to attend the king and his high-ranking companions. Even horribly ill and clinging to a chamber pot, the fresh-faced, twenty-year-old king had amused her with his wry jests and impressed her with his thoughtful questions about herbs and tonics and teas.

With careful treatment, she'd managed to bring every single man safely through their illness. Days later they had been sprightly enough to hear the loyalty pledges, and accept the surrender of the insurrectionist, John MacDonald, Lord of the Isles. The king had praised her skill and publicly announced he was in her debt. They had corresponded twice-monthly since then, and James often asked about improved methods of wound care or if she had a new salve recipe to send him. Of course, he hadn't officially repaid his debt until the royal tourney, and while she would always value his friendship and forever hold him in her prayers for ensuring the happiness of her children...she had no desire to bed him. James was thirty-two summers to her forty-two, and she viewed him as a cherished and slightly exasperating younger brother, not a potential lover.

Unlike Keir, who could make her wet with a look. Or a growl.

"I do appreciate your letters," Maude replied eventually.

"They were certainly a comfort in my bad marriage, and still make me smile."

James squeezed her hand, his gaze intent. "You're a widow now—"

"More wine, Your Grace?"

Startled at the unexpected and rather bold interruption, Maude glanced up to see Ida MacTier standing in front of the top table. The elder held a full jug of wine, but the glint of mischief in her eyes was far more concerning. Why, of all the clan members who had offered to assist with the banquet, did it have to be Ida serving them? The woman who had witnessed her and Keir together in the mountain dwelling and claimed they shot love sparks at each other?

Argh.

The king looked mildly irritated. "No, thank you madam."

"My lady?"

"Er...yes. Please," she replied, holding out her goblet.

Ida beamed. "I just poured for young Sorcha and her uncle. How well Keir's leg is progressing! Barely a limp now. Must be all those special treatments you've been providing in the apothecary."

Her cheeks hot enough to boil water, Maude gulped back the contents of the goblet, then held it out for more. If heavenly rescue from an amorous young king came this day in the form of a blunt-speaking grandmother, so be it.

"Coneflower salve," she burst out. "It turns the skin quite purple, but heals in miraculous ways, praise be to God."

"Well, be sure to keep treating him," said Ida. "It puts a skip in both your steps."

"Thank you," she said, a little taken aback at the approval. Perhaps not everyone believed the laird's widow needed to sit in a corner and wilt. And if Ida could be persuaded, perhaps the rest of the clan might be turned to that way of thinking as well. "That will be all."

When the woman nodded and moved along to fill other goblets, James leaned close once more. "I see it does not matter which great hall I am in, there is always an elder to comment on things that do not concern them. We'll speak in private after the banquet."

Maude's heart sank. "Of course, Your Grace."

Not long after, the second course was brought in. This time there were wheels of cheese, vegetable pottage, a dressed goose, jellies, pies and pastries, almonds and dried fruit, but Maude waved each dish away, her appetite gone. While James enjoyed a selection of pastries and cheeses, she took the opportunity to watch Keir. Her lover was eating a pie, and next to him, Sorcha was stuffing handfuls of dried fruit and sweetmeats into her girdle.

Look at me, Keir.

As though he'd heard her silent plea, Keir glanced over. Maddeningly, his face could have been carved from hewn rock and revealed nothing whatsoever. What was he thinking right now? Had he, in turn, been observing her and James? Had any part of their conversation carried to him? Perhaps he truly did believe that she and the king had been lovers. Heaven knew her late husband had made a fool of himself, swaying between thunderous temper and strutting like a peacock over her mercy ride to Dunstaffrage Castle.

Frustration overwhelmed her. Much like with Donald, she would have to walk the cliff edge of a noblewoman's duty with James, and even the thought wearied her after days of bliss with Keir during which she'd had the freedom to explore and revel in her own desires. Every touch, every act, had always been her choice. But freedom in private was no longer enough, not when she wanted so much more: to love Keir publicly and have him proudly by her side at this table as well as in her bed.

The banquet's second course seemed to last one hundred

years, but at last the empty dishes were carried back to the kitchens, and the trestle tables moved against the walls to allow space for music and dancing. While her sons and daughter-in-law assisted the hastily assembled minstrels in tuning their instruments, Maude's feet tapped impatiently, eager to begin. Right now, the top table felt like a cage rather than a position of honor, and dancing might be the only opportunity she had to speak with Keir this evening.

If she dared to defy the king.

He'd been banished for punching the old laird. He would die for punching the king. And yet his fingers still twitched to curl into a fist and knock James Stewart on his royal arse for the amount of hand holding and smiling occurring at the top table.

Keir leaned against the hall's south wall, the best place to stand for it kept a great many people between him and their reigning monarch. Naturally, the king was an excellent dancer, his steps light and surefooted as he twirled Maude around in a traditional Scottish reel with Callum and Lady Isla. Everyone was having a grand time, clapping their hands and stomping their feet to the music; the hall a mass of colorful clothing as members of the clan embraced the opportunity for amusement after the solemn statement taking here this morning.

"Evening, Keir. Good to see ye."

"Evening," he replied, although the two shepherds had already hurried past him, clearly eager to join the buxom dairymaids who were waiting on the next reel. Ach. Young lust. Brash, hopeful, and without a single clue. It couldn't possibly compare to the pleasures of bedding a mature woman, although perhaps fucking Maude was so good because he had deeper feelings for her.

Deeper feelings he could explore further if the damned king wasn't in the way.

"Will ye dance, Uncle?"

He glanced at his niece, who swayed on her tip-toes. "Ye know I do not."

Sorcha stared back beseechingly. "But I cannae see anything. Will ye lift me up? Then I'll be taller than everyone."

"Oh, verra well," he grumbled. "One turn about the hall and then I willnae hear one more peep about it, agreed?"

"Agreed!" she replied happily, holding out her arms.

Keir crouched, lifted the bairn, and settled her on his shoulder. When he stood to his full height, Sorcha shrieked in delight then rewarded his indulgence by covering and uncovering his eyes and rumpling his hair.

Ugh. How did mothers and fathers not lose their sweet minds?

"Here now," he said, tugging her toes. "Behave yourself."

She giggled and proceeded to tickle his nose with a lock of hair.

Keir shook his head. It was a blessing indeed he'd fathered no bairns over the years. This one of Burke's was enough mischief for any clan.

Continuing his amble along the walls so they avoided the dancers, Keir nodded as more people greeted them. While some remained cool—those who believed violence toward a laird to be wrong no matter what the circumstances—most of the clan had welcomed his return. He halted briefly to shake hands with some of the MacIntyre guard; they all wanted to know when he would return to the fold. At least his cut leg excused him for a while. Despite Callum's offer of his old cottage in the village or a dwelling on the castle grounds, he couldn't be this close to Maude without having her next to him. And that required a far better plan than continually injuring himself to gain admittance to the apothecary. Unlike his mountain dwelling, there was no privacy for secret or discreet visits in the village, not with so many others around. And as had been clearly demonstrated today, Maude sat high above him, no matter how often he claimed her.

That was a bitter tonic to swallow.

"Good evening, Sorcha. What a fine oak tree you have to sit in. And it walks, too!"

As his niece laughed, Keir gazed at Maude. She was beautiful. Just...*beautiful*. And merry from wine if her pink cheeks, bright eyes, and loud voice told a truthful tale. "Lady."

Her smile faltered a little, then she straightened her shoulders. "As you haven't yet asked me to dance, Keir Wright, I thought I would come and ask you."

"I dinnae dance," he said gruffly. "My leg...ow, bairn!"

Sorcha smiled angelically, as though she hadn't just pinched him. "That leg is much better, Uncle. Lady Maude fixed it with the purple salve so ye owe her a dance. Put me down on that bench over there."

Scowling, Keir dropped the wee redheaded devil onto the wooden bench. Then he coughed. "Would ye care to dance, Lady Maude?"

"Yes," she said simply, resting her hand on his sleeve as the minstrels struck up a new but thankfully familiar tune on pipe and lute.

He concentrated fiercely on the opening movements: hands clasped, step in and out twice, then two paces left. In and out twice, then two paces right. Not too difficult, he could manage those. Two claps. Aye, even that. Arms about each other's waist and a slow spin? Hmmm.

"Forgive me," he muttered, as his arm settled across her lush breasts rather than her waist, and he had to swiftly drop it.

"Wicked Highlander," Maude replied. "Making me want you again when I'm still tender from before."

Keir stumbled, cursing. "Shhh."

They each clapped twice, then Maude curled her arm about his waist, her wrist briefly brushing his cock. "Beg pardon. How clumsy of me."

His gaze narrowed as they began another slow spin. "Are ye teasing me or making the king jealous? Neither is a sound plan, angel."

"Oh? What might happen?" she asked, her eyes gleaming. "You'll pinch something sensitive? Dive deep for a pearl? Dear me. Such terrible punishments."

Keir grimaced; his cock throbbing, fingers itching, and mouth watering to do exactly those things. "How much wine have ye had to drink?"

"Not enough, clearly. We're still suffering a language barrier."

Again, they each stepped in and out, and he inwardly groaned at the endless dance. Another bloody clap, then their arms down to spin each other once more.

"Maude," he said warningly, when her hand cupped his arse.

She beamed. "That growl! I suggest a little honey on the tongue to sweeten your temper."

Keir bent his head to speak directly in her ear. "Ye think I won't punish ye for this willfulness? Think again."

"Yes. I'd best be careful, or you might spank my bottom. Even fuck it. Oh no!"

All the air whooshed from his lungs. Keir flexed his arm, fully intending to toss Maude over his shoulder and march out of the hall, laird and king and other clan members be damned. But the minstrels finished their tune with a flourish, and he had to bow to her instead. She was daft to tease him when he'd imagined spanking and fucking her rounded arse since the day they'd first met. *Daft.*

"Maude," he began. "I—"

"Master Wright!" said the king jovially as the crowd parted like curtains to let him through. "You've kept my dear friend from me long enough. Lady Maude, shall we walk?"

Do not punch the king. DO NOT PUNCH THE KING OF SCOTLAND.

Keir inhaled slowly to calm himself. This was a humbling reminder of an old lesson: height and brawn mattered naught against absolute power. For all his smiles and gifts and jests, the king could bed whomever he wanted, whenever he wanted. And there wasn't anything a poor commoner like Keir Wright could do about it. He had no legal claim over Maude.

"Best go, lady," he muttered, the words poisoning his tongue. "His Grace takes precedence over a lowly sword-fighter. Much better boots."

"My boots are fine, although we may be equals in clothing. I must visit the MacIntyre weaving house before I leave," said James, gracious in victory. "Lady Maude?"

Maude hesitated, and for one wild moment Keir thought she might refuse. But she placed her hand on the royal sleeve, then they turned and walked out the great hall's wide open double doors. The king's guards followed with polite disinterest, no doubt well used to this, but every member of Clan MacIntyre watched with wide eyes and loud whispers.

A roaring sound filled his ears, and Keir clenched his fists.

No. This was not how this night was supposed to end.

With a feral snarl Keir marched toward the doors, shouldering his way through the fray, uncaring if he separated dancers or spilled ale or knocked others on their arse. He had to get to Maude. Under no circumstances could she bed the king. Not now, not ever again. She was the only woman he'd ever loved, would ever love, and she belonged to him.

He charged down the hallway. Ahead was the private staircase leading to the castle's best guest chamber, where the king was staying.

"Master Wright."

Keir ignored the sharp words and suddenly found himself shoved against a cold stone wall, three sword tips at his throat. Bloody damned banquet. If he had his own sword rather than just a dagger at his hip, these three pups would each be short a hand.

"Ye don't understand," he snarled. "The lady is *mine*."

One of the king's guards shook his head, something akin to pity in his eyes. "Easy now. She'll be yours again tomorrow. Just not this night."

"Aye," said the second guard gently. "Not this night."

"Don't force our swords," said the third guard. "We have no desire to harm you, Master Wright. But we will if you take another step."

Keir glared at the men, sick with rage. They stared back impassively.

Eventually he swore, his head thumping against the stone wall. The three sword tips lowered, and the guards continued on their way.

God's blood.

Banishment had hurt, but a nobleman humbling him once again because he dared to have feelings for Lady Maude MacIntyre hurt infinitely worse.

And now he would return to the great hall, alone once more.

CHAPTER 9

"Wine, Maude?"

She turned from examining a unicorn tapestry in the gold chamber—apart from the laird's room, the most lavish in the castle and reserved for high-ranking guests—and glared at the King of Scotland. "Only if you care to wear it, Your Grace."

James slowly set down the pewter jug. "Is something amiss?"

"Yes. This attempted seduction or whatever you wish to call it," snapped Maude, thoroughly irritated with all the men in her life. James, who thought that being king meant every woman wanted him. Keir, who had just let her go without so much as an argument. Callum and Alastair for loving Isla so much they had been sharing a kiss in the corner of the great hall and thus missed the conversation between Keir and the king. Bah.

"Blunt words again? I did not think I was so bad at seduction."

"You are king. For most, that would be seduction enough."

James's wince almost made her regret her words. Almost. "But not for you? Very well. Perhaps you might offer guidance. How does a man go about wooing Lady Maude MacIntyre?"

Now that was a question without an easy answer. Keir had done so by just...well, being Keir. Of course, it helped that his brawn, height, and dark-haired good looks was an exceedingly attractive combination alongside his gifts in the art of pleasure. But being reunited with him in private had shown her so much more. A man who listened and discussed, who always spoke his gruff but goodhearted truth. A lover who never judged or ignored her desires, nor wanted her to be someone she wasn't. A protector who kept her safe without restricting her activities, who admired and encouraged her healing skills and remained unbothered by her visions. Since childhood, she had dreamed of someone to share her true self with. Not just a lover but a life companion, a meeting of souls like her own mother and father had enjoyed.

Keir was that someone.

Maude sighed and slumped onto a pile of oversized velvet cushions. "I'm afraid any attempt at seduction would be a futile effort, Your Grace. Not because you aren't handsome or learned or brave or charming, but because my heart is engaged elsewhere."

"Ah," said the king, ambling over to sit beside her. "Keir Wright."

A blush swept across her cheeks. "I admired him from the day we met. Those feelings grew and grew until Donald forbade me from tending Keir, even speaking to him. Then he was banished and my heart broke in two. But after his leg injury we were reunited at last, and I have learned so many things about him. About myself. How it feels to have a man who cares deeply for me rather than what I can gain him. A man who is most proficient at, er..."

"Fucking?" said James, with a smirk. "Many claim the talent yet so few truly possess it. I have no need to brag; my reputation precedes me. But my dove, you must have a care for his knees."

She snorted. "And mine."

"Well, you are to be a grandmother."

"Disrespect a crone at your peril, *laddie*."

"I would not dare! But your words suggest that I shan't receive so much as a pity bedding from my old friend?" James asked lightly, a wicked glint in his eyes.

"You have two hands, Your Grace. Now, if you behave, I may bestow a sisterly hug. Then I'll tell you how remarkably successful fat snails, infusions of yarrow, and coneflower salve were in the treatment of a nasty cut…"

Several hours later, when she'd consumed more goblets of wine and the topics of wounds, herbals, and lovelorn kings had been exhausted, Maude strolled back down the torch-lit hallways to her own bedchamber. The castle was quiet; the banquet and entertainment in the great hall long finished and the clan members departed for their own dwellings. In fact, the only people awake and alert were the king's guards, and the MacIntyre warriors on duty. Not that it mattered who saw her. Every single person who watched her leave the hall on James's arm would assume she had bedded him, even if they both denied it with their last breath.

Entering her chamber, she closed the door behind her and rested against it. Unwilling to wake a waiting woman at this hour, Maude took off her jewel-studded girdle before yanking on the ties fastening her gown sleeves to release them. After much fumbling and colorful words, she managed to undo the two buttons at her nape and remove her silver gown, then discard her kirtle, until all she wore was a simple linen shift. Yes, it was late and she'd had enough wine this evening to launch a warship, but her empty bed held no appeal. And after discussing healing arts with the king for so long, she didn't particularly want to go to her apothecary either. Instead, her gaze rested on the adjoining door between her chamber and Keir's.

Did she dare go in?

Her feet began walking, answering that question well enough.

Slowly, with the care only an intoxicated person could take, Maude opened the door and crept into Keir's chamber. Soon her knee connected sharply with the edge of a low table, but she managed to stifle her howl of pain into a small squeak. Until two steps later, when she stumbled against a chair and bumped that same knee. Ack! Where had all this furniture come from? It was literally leaping into her path.

"Lady Maude, what are ye doing?"

She stilled at Sorcha's sleepy question and glanced sideways at the oversized four poster bed, partially illuminated by three candles. The little girl was curled up at the end of it, wrapped from head to toe in her primrose blanket. Keir was also awake and sitting up in bed, his massive arms folded, watching her with a narrowed gaze.

Sitting up in bed *shirtless*.

Maude fought the urge to pounce on him like a cat. "Er... good evening. Just wanted to look in here and see if you were both well."

"Really?" said Keir.

She hiccupped and covered her mouth. "Really," she mumbled.

"Lady Maude," said Sorcha, giggling. "Did ye drink a whole barrel of wine?"

"I don't believe so," said Maude, trying to remember. "The king also had many goblets."

Keir scowled. "Ye came here to speak of him?"

"No. I've been talking and talking since we left the great

hall, about wounds and salves and the heavy burden of a crown, and I don't wish to talk about James anymore."

"Just...talking?"

"Just talking," said Maude, peering at Keir in confusion because now there were two of him sitting side by side in bed. "Not sure why you're so irritable though, when you just let me go like some sort of Highland blockhead."

"Uncle is a blockhead sometimes, but he means well," said Sorcha earnestly.

"A blockhead for a moment," Keir growled. "Then I came after ye."

Warmth infused her to the tips of her toes. "You did?"

"Aye. And I got three sword tips to the throat for my trouble."

Maude bit her lip and climbed onto the bed, before awkwardly crawling up to sit beside him. "Do not fret, I'm here to treat you."

"Oh?"

"It is quite obvious," she said, kissing his cheeks and forehead and neck, even each eyelid, "that you are a patient in urgent need of tender care."

Keir grunted. Yet he didn't pull away.

Cupping his jaw, reveling in the scratch of his beard against her fingers, Maude traced his lips with her thumb. Teasing. Then she leaned down and kissed him softly. Not a kiss to inflame passion...but a promise of so much more.

"Ugh," said Sorcha, wrinkling her nose. "You really did want to kiss him, just like Grandmother Ida said."

Maude nodded and yanked back the linen sheet and quilt. "'Tis true. Now I'm going to hug him because your uncle had a very trying evening. But I need your help. He requires so many hugs."

Keir's eyes widened, but it was too late. Sorcha emerged from her blanket cocoon and nearly catapulted herself next to him before throwing one bony arm across his chest and patting it. Maude twined herself around his other side like a vine, her head on his shoulder. He didn't say a word, merely pulled up the quilt to cover them all. Then one paw-hand came to rest on Sorcha's back, and one on hers.

Ah. Perfect.

"I'm verra tired," said Sorcha, her eyes already closed.

"Me too," said Maude, sighing happily as Keir's fingers began stroking her hair, the warmth of his body utterly delicious against hers.

"Sleep, angel."

So she did.

Several hours later, Maude yelped when the bed moved. Her eyes flew open to learn that Keir was carrying her back to her own chamber, and she hissed in disapproval when he gently laid her down on cold sheets.

"I wish I could stay with you," she whispered. "I don't want to love only in private."

Keir leaned down and kissed her so rawly, so roughly, that it curled her toes. "Soon. When the investigation is complete and the criminal vanquished, I swear, you'll wake in my bed each morning. I'll convince the laird. Somehow."

Maude nodded, trying to remain cheerful. Just because those two obstacles loomed larger than Ben Cruachan, did not mean they were impossible.

Surely.

Maude had chosen him over the king.

Even now, after another hour's sleep, mass in the chapel, and breakfast in the great hall, Keir could barely believe it. The news was so momentous he wanted to unfurl a banner from the ramparts, or send a town crier to the center of the village, but he wouldn't breathe a word. This was a secret to hold close to his heart until the right time, when he could prove himself to the laird and declare their match publicly.

A future with Maude and him and Sorcha together as a family would be rosy indeed. Even if it did involve bony bairn elbows and being called a Highland blockhead.

Keir's lips twitched. His woman was indeed saucy with a belly full of wine, but such memories ensured he could hold his peace as they stood in the courtyard to farewell the king. Hell, he could even smile as James kissed Lady Isla and Maude on the cheek, shook hands with Callum and Alastair, and mounted his horse so easily.

Then the king halted. "Master Wright!"

Surprised at the sudden hail, he marched over. "Your Grace?"

"Treat her well or you'll have me to answer to and next time my guards won't be so courteous with their blade tips," said James, his gaze flint hard.

Keir merely nodded. This was the king conceding defeat; it certainly wasn't the time to argue his superior sword skill. "I swear."

"By the by, I was pondering Glennoe's investigation and how oddly unfortunate the Wright family has been. A banishment, then the raid that took your kin and destroyed the weaving house, now the fire on the mountain."

"Aye," Keir replied cautiously.

"Something that perplexed me: even without royal banner or large procession, the borderlands watchtower saw my approach, which provoked the clan's chain of signals and riders. Yet that didn't happen with either the Campbell raid or the attack on your home. That watchtower can see for miles. It would be impossible to miss a daylight raiding party or someone wandering about the clearing with chains and a fire striker. Unless of course...the guard wasn't there."

A cold chill gripped Keir like a sodden cloak. "Or the guard on duty saw and did nothing. Two men could not neglect their duty so badly, surely. But one man with a grudge against me, perhaps yes."

The king inclined his head, then gripped his horse's reins. "I wish you well on your journey to truth and justice, Master Wright."

Keir dropped to one knee. "God bless and keep ye, Your Grace."

"And you. Cruachan!"

With that, their sovereign turned his horse in an enviably smooth arc, and cantered away toward the mountain, his guards closely behind.

Keir remained in the courtyard, his stomach churning with rage. The Campbell raid had never sat right with him due to the ease of the attack. But his mind had gone to secret paths and shelters. What if it was far simpler than that? A borderlands watchtower guard who ignored danger when it suited him?

He needed to find out who had been on duty this week, and back in August.

"Keir? Are you well?"

He turned to see Callum approaching, Maude right behind her son. "After a discussion with the king, I must ask a boon."

The laird's gaze sharpened. "Oh?"

"Donald MacIntyre wasn't a scholar, but ye are a learned man. Are records kept about the clan beyond births, deaths, and marriages? Anything about guards and their duties?"

"Yes," said Callum slowly. "I keep note each week so no guard is unfairly burdened with too many night watches. Why do you ask?"

"I wondered who might have been in the border tower this week. Also the week of the raid. For they somehow managed to miss a party of Campbells *and* a criminal wandering about with chains and a large steel fire striker."

Maude gasped. "Gavin MacTier is on duty this week. Heather told me when she gave her statement in the great hall. What if he was responsible the week of the raid as well?"

"The answer to that lies in the record chamber," said the laird grimly. "Let us go find it."

They hurried back to the castle, gathering Lady Isla, Alastair, and Sorcha on the way. Yet Keir could barely breathe as one name clawed itself into his mind with the might of a golden eagle's talon.

Gavin MacTier.

The man who had replaced him as captain of the guard. Chosen not because Gavin was the best or bravest fighter... but because he had near-worshiped Donald and obeyed orders without question, no matter what those orders were. It seemed that devotion did not extend to Callum, though, for the new laird's invitation for Keir to return to the village had not been delivered the first time or the second.

Gavin bloody MacTier.

Keir's fingers itched to unsheathe his sword and cleave the man in half. But he had to wait for the last few pieces of evidence first. A mindless butcher he was not.

Yet.

"What are we doing, Uncle?" whispered Sorcha as she ran up the narrow, circular staircase to keep pace with his long stride. The records chamber was on the first floor, next to the laird's library.

"Going to look at some books, bairn," he replied. "Books that might hold a clue to explain all the verra bad luck we've been having."

"Spell books?"

"Nae, record books."

She went quiet then, and Keir could practically see her

mind turning over in confusion. But they were nearly there, and he only just stopped himself from dropping a shoulder and bursting through the oak door like a battering ram.

Callum pushed it open and walked into the small, very clean, records chamber. It held a sea of leather-bound books on shelves, scrolls, piles of parchment, and wooden storage chests. "Good morning."

Two busy scribes, both dressed in a monk's simple tunic and cowl, leaped to their feet and bowed.

"Laird!" said one. "Are ye here for the statements?"

"No. I need guard record books. For the borderlands watchtower...August of last year."

"Of course. I shall fetch it."

It seemed to take a thousand years for the scribe to find the correct book; even calm, steady Callum was drumming his fingers on the table. Alastair looked ready to pull every book from the shelf, Lady Isla and Maude were pacing, and Sorcha was dipping her finger into an ink pot and swirling it on her arm. But at last the scribe returned, holding up a heavy tome before setting it onto a sloped reading bench.

"Here ye are, laird. Some pages can stick together, but a gentle fingernail will free them."

Keir glared at his own oversized hands compared to the scribe's slender, nimble ones. It was just as well he'd not been given this task; not only was he a poor reader, the record book might have ended up in pieces on the floor. But the laird merely nodded, expertly thumbing through the tome as he searched for the week of the raid. Then he trailed his fingertip down the side of a particular page, and halted.

"Hmmm."

"Hmmm? What is hmmm, my love?" said Lady Isla impatiently.

Callum smiled at the scribe, then stepped back from the

book. "Thank you for your assistance. We'll leave your precious records be and retire to my library."

Wanting to roar at the laird's discretion, Keir stormed to the adjacent room. When everyone stood inside and the door was latched shut for privacy, Callum spoke once more. "Gavin was on duty the week of the raid."

"No!" exclaimed Maude, her eyes flashing. "That unspeakable *wretch*."

Keir muttered an oath, only the presence of Lady Isla and Sorcha keeping him from doing far worse. He would find Gavin MacTier and tear the rat bastard apart, one limb at a time.

"Will ye lend me a horse, laird? So I might visit the MacTier dwelling?"

"Yes," said Callum. "But you'll not be going alone, Keir. It is my duty as laird to hear Gavin's testimony and decide his guilt or innocence in the matter. And his punishment."

"He could have killed Mau...your lady mother!" snarled Keir. "There is no worthy explanation for that!"

"I must still ask him why. I cannot allow your feelings—or my own—to cloud my judgement. Isla, perhaps you might stay with Sorcha—"

"Nae laird!" Sorcha burst out. "I have a dis...a disp..."

"A dispute," said Lady Isla as she rested a hand on Sorcha's shoulder and gave her husband a look that was part glare, part plea. "We will both come, but promise to stay out of the way."

"Miles out of the way," snapped Alastair.

"I shall also attend," said Maude firmly.

Keir froze. A part of him wished to shout *no*, that she could not go anywhere near danger. He could have lost her on the mountain, and the thought of Maude at risk again curdled his gut. But she was the clan healer. Not for the world would he clip his angel's wings. "You'll be verra, verra, *verra* careful."

"I promise," she replied, squeezing his hand and smiling at him.

Oh, how he loved her.

The laird coughed, his gaze narrowed. "We shall discuss certain other personal matters on our return. But for now, I'll dispatch guards to block the paths around the clearing. Let us gather some weapons and ride."

Keir nodded grimly. Indeed, today would be a reckoning for all things.

☙❧

Gavin MacTier!

Maude paused in repacking her herbal satchel, her hands shaking so badly with fury that the small glass bottles and pots were all on the verge of breaking.

That rat. That viper. That festering pile of excrement.

No doubt Keir had much better curses; she was nearly at a loss for words. But one question remained lodged in her mind: how could anyone be so filled with hate, so utterly without soul or qualm, that they could commit such terrible acts?

Such terrible *planned* acts.

None had been committed drunk on ale or in the heat of a fight, and that made Gavin very dangerous indeed. But that led to the second important question: *why*. What had Gavin gained from ignoring the Campbell raid? What grudge did he hold against his laird's mother, Keir, and young Sorcha, that made their deaths acceptable?

This was madness. Just madness. And with no vision to guide her or offer reassurance of the outcome, she was frightened beyond measure.

"Do ye need help with that satchel, angel?"

Maude threw herself against Keir's chest. His arms closed

tightly around her, so tightly she could scarcely breathe, but she craved that security right now. "You must also swear you'll be *verra verra verra careful*."

"I will. However, one thing I cannae promise is mercy, no matter what your son says. He must do as a laird should. But I am a man robbed of a brother and sister-in-law, of my home and theirs, and my niece has suffered terribly. Ye could have been snatched from me. Gavin's sins are too many in my eyes. Too many to live."

"I understand," she whispered. "But—"

A loud cough from the doorway interrupted her, and they both turned to see Isla beckoning them frantically. "Mother. Keir. The horses await."

"Yes," said Maude, reluctantly stepping back from him. "I was just packing my satchel...I thought a tonic to soothe Heather's babe would be a reason to visit their dwelling."

Isla nodded. "Good. Very good. Perhaps we can coax Ida, Heather, and the children from the dwelling while the men... er...all listen to Callum and do exactly as he bids," she finished pointedly.

Keir grunted, his hand resting on the sword hilt at his hip. "Lady."

That wasn't agreement, and both she and Isla knew it. But there was no time to argue. Maude hefted the satchel over her shoulder and adjusted the strap against her breasts. "Let us depart, then."

A quarter hour later, they were all atop their horses and away. She, Callum, Alastair, and Keir each had their own mount, while Sorcha sat in front of Isla. It might have been the quietest ride in Scottish history; they nodded at people as they passed through the bustling village, but did not halt to talk, too intent on reaching the MacTier dwelling. Even Sorcha held her tongue.

Although she knew guards had been dispatched, Maude's

gaze darted left and right as they rode along the wide dirt path toward the clearing at the foot of Ben Cruachan. Her mind was flooded with a thousand worries—if someone she loved would be hurt, if any of the guards would alert Gavin to their approach or perhaps even side with him in his cause. He did wield some power as captain of the guard, and although the man wasn't as naturally gifted or large in stature as Keir, he still possessed skill with sword in hand.

Maude shivered. It was just so hard to believe Gavin could hold such malice. He'd always been abrupt but not overtly rude. Yes, he'd certainly been Donald's man through and through—furious at the broken nose and perhaps a strong supporter of Keir's banishment for reasons other than his own position. But with the raid and the fires, such neglect of duty was impossible to explain.

When they were about one hundred feet or so from the MacTier dwelling, Callum held up his hand and they all came to a halt. "Lady Mother, Isla has informed me of your plan to take the tonic and find out information. I am reluctantly agreeable. But under no circumstances may any of you venture inside the dwelling if Gavin is there. We have no idea what he might do if he feels cornered."

Maude nodded. As she dismounted, her gaze met Keir's. He pressed his fingers to his lips in a discreet kiss, and it gave her the strength to continue and play her part. Those in the MacTier dwelling needed to believe two ladies and a child they knew well had arrived for a friendly visit to discuss mother and babe matters, nothing more.

Taking a deep breath for composure, she linked arms with Isla, took Sorcha's hand, and they walked up to the small stone dwelling. It was well-kept, with a neatly swept path, flower garden, and shutters painted blue. As Gavin was often away with guard duties, Ida and Heather worked admirably hard, especially with Craig and the newborn to tend as well.

Isla knocked on the dwelling door. Soon it swung open to reveal a rather grim-looking Ida. Behind her, Heather was trying to soothe her squalling babe.

"Oh!" said Ida, her face brightening. "Lady Maude. Lady Isla. And young Sorcha. Forgive us, we weren't expecting ye."

Maude glanced about, but there was no sign of Gavin, so she reached into her satchel and pulled out a bottle. "Good morning! No need for any fuss, this is a mercy visit. Forgive me for not coming sooner; I brought a tonic for your little one. To help him rest easy so you might have an hour's peace."

Heather looked up from the kitchen table, pure relief on her face. "Bless ye. I'm at my wit's end with this babe. He doesnae cry for breast or because of wet smallcloths...he just cries. And Gavin doesn't like me asking for help. Says I should know what to do."

"Poor dear," said Isla sympathetically. "It's all well and good for your husband, when he is out on the tower and away from the noise. Is he back soon?"

"He's back now," said a low, angry voice, then Heather's tall, lean husband entered the kitchen area. "And not happy to see visitors in his dwelling. What do ye women want?"

The back of Maude's neck prickled like a bad rash. Gavin's eyes were so cold and flat. The insult of viper fitted him very well indeed. "Good morning. I just gave Heather a tonic to help the babe sleep."

"We've no need of your spells, witch."

"What did you say to the clan healer?" asked Isla sharply, putting a restraining hand on Sorcha's shoulder.

Gavin moved closer, his fists clenching. "I think ye heard me well enough, Lady Isla. Now, why don't ye explain why you're really here?"

Maude glanced across at Ida and Heather. Both were staring at Gavin, their mouths agape.

"Husband," said Heather tentatively. "They came to help."

"Shut that fool mouth or I'll shut it for ye," snarled Gavin, cuffing the top of his wife's head so hard it jerked back. "We'll accept nothing from a devil-spawned witch."

Fury rose in Maude. Although Donald had never struck her, his temper and threats had haunted her for twenty-six years, and to know another clan wife suffered made her blood boil. As Lady of Glennoe, she'd had no one nearby to turn to for help. But Heather did.

"We did come to help, Heather," she said calmly. "Should you wish sanctuary for you and Ida and your children."

Gavin stormed forward, hatred clear on his face. "What? Ye think to steal my family from me like ye stole my father? I'll kill ye first!"

The words were so shocking, Maude faltered. Stole his father? How had she stolen Munro MacTier? They had exchanged pleasantries but nothing further, for the man had been a busy stonemason, building and repairing dwellings. "What on earth are you talking about? I barely knew Munro."

"Not *him*. My real father. Donald MacIntyre."

Utter silence fell in the cottage. Even the babe stopped wailing, and the sudden quiet was all the more eerie as a breeze rustled the trees outside. Were Keir and Callum and Alastair close by? Were they hearing this?

"What?" she said, her brow furrowing.

"It is not plain from my height and dark hair?" screamed Gavin. "Your husband was my father. My mother's sweetheart. But ye bewitched him! Then compelled that bastard Keir Wright to break his nose, and ensure he later withered and died!"

Stunned, Maude could only stare. But before she could gather her thoughts and respond, Gavin grabbed her arm and yanked it viciously behind her back. Sorcha flew forward and tried to kick his shin, but he easily flung her away. Isla grabbed the child and retreated to a corner.

"Let her go, Gavin," warned Isla. "Do not make this any worse."

"Ye heard the lady," said Keir as he shoved his way into the dwelling. "Let Maude go. Now."

Gavin laughed, the sound like chains scraping on rock, and suddenly the icy point of a dagger pressed against Maude's throat. "I don't think so. But it's good you're all here. Now the truth can be told...and I'll have my proper revenge at last."

CHAPTER 10

Removing Gavin MacTier's limbs one at a time was too kind a death for what he'd done. Perhaps a few turns on the water wheel would be better, or even hung, drawn, and quartered. And for each moment the man held that dagger to Maude's throat, his impending death would only become grislier.

Keir gulped in air, a futile attempt to quell his rage. But he couldn't do anything just yet. The dwelling was small and there were too many people in it to start slashing a sword about. He needed to lure Gavin outside somehow, where the laird and Alastair and the other guards waited.

Perhaps this foolishness about being the old laird's son was key.

"Ye claim to be Donald's son, Gavin?"

Ida snorted. "I dinnae ken where he heard that tale from, but his head is full of rocks to believe it."

Gavin stomped his foot. "The laird told me himself, Mother! That ye were sweethearts before this witch came north, and I was borne in secrecy. Donald couldnae claim me as a lad because of his wife's friendship with the king. But he said he was proud of me! That is why I was appointed captain...it was my birthright!"

"Oh, my son, ye have heard twisted truths from a forked tongue," said Ida, shaking her head. "I was a tavern wench, paid good coin to lie with Donald because I was older. Experienced. No lass his age or equal to his rank wanted to be near him; they already knew his cruel temper. That is why the laird traveled all the way to England for a bride. We weren't sweethearts, and he certainly wasn't your father. The only man I loved and had a child with was Munro MacTier, may his blessed soul rest in peace. Anything ye have done dishonors him. And me. And your wife and bairns. Have ye acts to confess, Gavin?"

Keir's hand tightened on his sword. Most men accused of serious crimes at least knew to hold their peace, but Gavin seemed in a boastful mood. If they could extract a confession from him, perhaps that would meet the laird's requirements for a fair hearing. "I dinnae understand the raid. How ye convinced the Campbells to raze the weaving house."

Gavin's lip curled. "Of course ye don't understand, with all that common Wright blood."

"Ye have common MacTier blood," snapped his mother.

"Liar! But I'll answer the question. It was the perfect plan. With the weaving house and income gone, the MacIntyres would starve. Then the Campbells could get rid of the weak halfling laird and his witch mother, and claim the fertile land they've always wanted. They promised riches aplenty."

Maude lifted her chin. "You failed in every way."

"Not every way, madam," said Gavin, pressing the dagger harder against her throat until a trickle of blood appeared. "It hurt Keir. I could have killed him easily enough, but killing those he loved while he was far away and helpless...so much better."

A primitive snarl rumbled in Keir's chest. Gavin dared to

hurt Maude? And the way he was so proud of his acts! Oh, he was going to enjoy disemboweling this madman. "Why the fire?"

"Donald's wife was *forbidden* to tend or speak to ye. She should have stayed away. But she dishonored the laird's memory and went up the mountain. I couldnae permit a traitor and a witch to be together. Ye both should have died, along with the brat."

Heather began to cry. "Husband, no. That is evil ye speak."

"I thought I told ye to shut that fool mouth," hissed Gavin.

Keir straightened his shoulders. "'Tis plain and simple ye are not the old laird's son."

"*What?*"

"Donald MacIntyre at least fought face to face. Ye conspire with another clan. Creep about in the shadows with chains and fire striker. Hit your wife. Hold a dagger to a lady's throat. Ye are naught but a sniveling coward, Gavin."

"I am not!" the other man shouted.

"Then fight me," said Keir, holding his gaze. "If ye can kill me so easily, prove it. Outside with swords, just the two of us. Show everyone this noble blood ye claim and defeat the commoner."

Once again, all fell quiet in the dwelling. So quiet, the thump of his heartbeat sounded as loud as a drum. In the corner, there came a hastily muffled gasp from Sorcha, but Keir did not turn away from Gavin. The wretched bastard was tempted. So poisoned with hate that he truly thought to win the day, even after everything he'd done.

After an endless wait, Gavin smiled and shoved Maude forward so she fell to her knees. "Verra well. Kiss the traitor farewell, witch. He'll not see the sunset. We'll meet next in the clearing."

Keir quickly reached down to help Maude to her feet. Sorcha ran forward, throwing her arms around him, then the three of them followed Isla from the dwelling. Just outside the door, Callum and Alastair waited impatiently, and they pulled Isla into a bear-like hug.

"Did ye hear enough, laird?" growled Keir.

"I did," said Callum, his face starkly pale.

"Will ye stop me?"

"No. A duel to the death is an honorable offer. I wish you well."

Keir turned to Maude. Her eyes were sheened with tears... but not of fear or fright, just a love so powerful it could not be contained. Pure warmth flowed through him. "Will ye offer a blessing, angel?"

"Of course," she said hoarsely.

He dropped to one knee. When her slender hands rested on his head and she murmured words he could not understand, that warmth increased tenfold and settled around him like sturdy armor. Now he near-itched to fight.

Keir rose and discarded his doublet and shirt.

"Uncle!"

"Bairn?"

Sorcha yanked the yellow ribbon from her hair, then tied it around his wrist. "Kill him dead."

"Aye," Keir replied, stroking her cheek.

A gust of wind whipped through the clearing, making those around him shiver. Utterly unbothered, Keir unsheathed his sword and stalked to where Gavin waited. The other man was also shirtless, but his teeth were audibly chattering.

"Whatever is the matter, Gavin?" asked Keir with a feral smile. "Cold?"

Bellowing an oath, Gavin charged forward and slashed his sword left and right. At the first shriek of blade on blade,

Keir nearly roared his joy as he easily deflected the blows. Donald's banishment might have denied him, but he was *born* for this, at one with the longsword in his hand.

Keir smiled as Gavin continued to bob and weave around him, merely sidestepping when required. Let the rat bastard tire himself out.

"I'll kill ye," said Gavin, already sucking in deeper breaths.

"Come on then, laddie. Do it. Serve up my innards on a platter."

Gavin charged again, lifting his arms in a wide arc as he swung his blade with great force horizontally in an attempt to remove Keir's head. But Keir blocked the blow with a straight blade, then countered with a thrust that opened a cut on Gavin's belly.

The other man faltered, actually halting to stare at the oozing blood before raising his sword once more and swinging wildly at Keir in an upward thrust.

"The witch fucked the king," panted Gavin, his eyes bulging with his efforts. "Over and over. Said James was the best lover she'd ever had."

Tiresome wretch.

Keir feinted to the left, then swung hard from the right and down, the blade slicing his enemy's thigh.

Gavin sank to his knees as blood spurted from the wound, his sword falling harmlessly away. "I liked it," he wheezed, "when your family died. They screamed...but ye weren't there."

A strange calmness washed over Keir, draining the rage and agonizing grief that he'd carried for so long and infusing him with unnatural strength.

Do it, brother. Avenge us.

The words were no more than a whisper in the wind, but Keir nodded. Aye. It was time to end this.

Gripping Gavin by the throat to hold him still, Keir

stabbed his blade deeply into the other man's stomach and twisted it. "For Burke. May he rest in peace."

Then he withdrew the blade, stabbed hard again, and twisted. "For Fiona. May she rest in peace."

A terrible gurgling sound escaped Gavin's mouth as he fell back onto the ground. Keir grimaced, part of him wanting his enemy to suffer more. But unlike Gavin, he wasn't soulless. Death would be swift, not lingering.

Slashing with his blade, he cut Gavin's throat. Then, with a low snarl, he buried his sword tip in the ground as another gust of wind swirled around him, lifting his hair and caressing his skin. Cleansing him.

His vengeance was complete.

"Keir. Keir!"

"Uncle!"

The words were shrieked from his left, then two bodies threw themselves against him. He leaned down, cupping Maude's cheek and kissing her fiercely. Then he lifted Sorcha up onto his hip.

She wrapped her thin arms about his neck. "I love ye, Uncle. Can we go home now?"

Tears blurred his vision. "Where is that, bairn?" he asked gruffly.

"At the castle. Us together with Lady Maude."

Maude hugged them both. "Aunt Maude."

Sorcha sniffled. "I suppose I could call ye that."

Overcome with emotion, Keir had to breathe deeply to compose himself. He had defeated his enemy. Broken down the walls between him and his niece. But greatest of all, he held the woman he loved in his arms. "Angel..."

Maude brushed her lips against his bare chest, marking him as hers. "I know," she said softly. "I know."

Gavin MacTier was dead. They were all now safe from his mad wrath.

Maude pressed a hand to her chest. It might take a while for her heart to stop pounding, though. Even with the ancient and powerful chant of protection she'd placed over Keir, fear had still gripped her during the swordfight, simply because she did not know the extent of the darkness he faced. But Gavin had no otherworldly power within him. He was just a man led astray by lies and jealousy and hate who would now be judged in purgatory for his acts.

Her mind still whirling, Maude watched Keir and her sons carefully carry Gavin's body back inside the dwelling, where Heather and Ida would wash and prepare it for burial. As a healer, death was never easy to witness, not when she worked so hard to prevent it. But on this occasion, there was such a sense of justice done, of ending one man's prolonged reign of remorseless crime, that she could not mourn his passing. All her sympathies were with Ida and Heather and the boys. It would be a very difficult time for them, reconciling the flawed man they knew with the heinous acts he'd confessed to. At least Callum would ensure they didn't suffer for Gavin's sins; she'd heard him offer food and coin and a cottage in the village if they wished.

Maude hesitantly walked up to Ida. Neither she nor Heather had screamed or wailed when Gavin had fallen, the two women had merely held each other. Craig had wept a little when he'd first seen his father's lifeless form, but was now running around the clearing with Sorcha. "Is there anything I can do, Ida? Do you need rosemary for the water or fabric for a shroud?"

The elder shook her head. "Nae, lady, we have some. But I would appreciate ye asking the priest to say a mass for Gavin's soul...ach, do not fret for us. I lost my son many years ago."

"How do you mean?"

"He wasnae a loving husband to Heather or a good father to the boys. Gavin was devoted only to Donald, then the memory of Donald. We will rest easier from this day forward with a peaceful household. Tell Keir...I hold no ill-will in my heart for the swordfight. It was a far more honorable death than my son deserved. I just hope Keir can forgive me for not knowing that Gavin had committed such grave sins."

"None of us knew," said Maude firmly.

"When he held a dagger to your neck...ach. It was frightening indeed. There was such madness in his eyes...tell me ye dinnae believe that foolishness about him being Donald's son. It is a lie, I swear."

"I don't believe it. Donald told countless lies and wielded threats like an axe; he liked to set people against each other and watch the disorder unfold. It amused him. With Gavin admiring Donald so, it would have been easy to turn his mind with untruths that contained a sprinkling of facts. As for having to bed Donald, I know exactly the awfulness of that task."

Unexpectedly, Ida smiled. "Aye. But my Munro was a wonderful lover. He healed my heart. Keir is a good man, let him heal yours."

"He already has," said Maude, smiling in return.

"Then for the love of Christ, wed him before ye are trampled by an army of wenches all eager to welcome his cock back to the village."

She laughed. "I will."

Not long after that, she, Keir, Callum, Alastair, and Isla were on their horses and ready to depart the clearing. Sorcha whispered that she wished to ride with her aunt. Touched at the shy request, Maude agreed.

Surprisingly, the chilly breeze had died away, and the noon sun was attempting to push through the clouds and shine on Glennoe. This time the ride would be a pleasant one; a gentle amble where they could inhale the fresh scent of wildflowers and admire the magnificent, imposing sight of Ben Cruachan against the pale blue sky.

Maude lifted her face to the heavens, wishing she was naked at her prayer window and feeling the strengthening warmth on her whole body. She had much to give thanks for, even if the small dagger cut on her neck was a little tender.

Nothing a kiss from her beloved couldn't fix, though.

As though he'd heard the thought, Keir turned his head from where he rode beside her and grinned. "Soon, angel."

"Beg pardon?" she replied, feigning surprise. "I did not make a request."

"I have a request, though," said Isla. "No, actually it is more of a command as the Lady of Glennoe. When can I expect your return to the guards, Keir? They need a new captain, and based on what I saw of your sword arm this day, I have decided it must be you."

"Ye wish that?" said Keir. "High praise indeed from the best in Scotland."

"Well...I mean your footwork could be improved..."

Isla's husbands groaned in unison.

"Please," said Callum, as he pulled up his horse, blocking the path back to the castle. "No talk of footwork today. Let us speak of other matters. Such as...the fact that our lady mother and a warrior have been meeting in private without the benefit of priest or holy sacrament."

Maude pursed her lips. While she very much wanted to wed Keir, priest and holy sacrament was another matter entirely. Even the thought of a chapel ceremony, one in a darkened room with incense burning and a clergyman gesturing while reciting in Latin, made her insides shrivel. It did not have to be that way. Not when in Scotland there was the wonderful, blissful, *legal* custom of irregular marriages that did not require a priest or posting of the banns at all.

This was certainly something to be discussed with Keir at a later time...although knowing he shared her distaste for the chapel, she was quite confident of convincing him that an irregular marriage was the answer.

"Er..." she began, shifting uncomfortably on her saddle.

"What are ye saying exactly, laird?" said Keir. "Is that a rebuke of your mother and me, or a demand to hear my intentions? Surely ye ken how I feel about her."

Callum blinked at the directness of the question. "Not a rebuke as such. We are all aware that even discreet private meetings are seen by someone, and in a castle, there are many someones. I won't have Mother called a whore to her face or behind her back. Witch was unpleasant enough. So, I must encourage a wedding. Very soon."

"Strongly encourage it," added Alastair, giving Keir a hard look. "A wedding before any further bedding."

"Bedding?" blurted Sorcha. "Dinnae be angry about that. Aunt Maude drank a barrel of wine, tripped over chairs, and kissed Uncle all over his face, but she meant well."

Maude pressed a fist to her lips so she didn't laugh. Fortunately, her sons and daughter-in-law didn't know all that had gone on in the mountain dwelling or behind closed castle doors, just as she didn't need to hear about their marital adventures. Not everything had to be shared. "They know, sweetling."

But Keir looked confused. As though sharing the emotion, his horse snorted and pawed at the dirt path. "Are ye saying then, laird, that the quarrel is not my inferior birth or position...but bedding before wedding?"

"You'll be captain of the guard," said Isla stoutly. "It is a position of honor. And the king approves of you, everyone saw you talking together. What really matters is Mother's happiness. It is quite clear you care for her and she cares for you."

Callum cleared his throat. "What I'm saying, is that there'll be no more prolonged apothecary treatments unless you're married."

"I'll approve when Mother's name is Lady Maude *Wright*," added Alastair, shooting Keir another look.

Maude rolled her eyes. Could they not at least have this overprotective son blather in the library with comfortable chaise, fireplace, and glasses of whisky, rather than on a dirt path surrounded by snow-capped mountains? Her bottom was becoming quite numb. Really, her children were behaving shamefully considering she was a woman of forty-two summers, soon to be a grandmother, and requiring many restorative kisses from her lover.

"Now that everyone has had their say," said Maude, adding a slight tremor to her voice for good measure, "perhaps we could continue back to the castle? I'm feeling a little weak. The cut to my neck..."

Keir made a sound of dismay, but she swiftly met his gaze and winked. He shook his head, his lips twitching. Hmmm. Perhaps it was still possible to be punished for saucy behavior. They would need to retire to her bedchamber as soon as possible to tend her *injury*.

"Forgive me, Mother," said Callum contritely. "Let us go home at once."

Maude nodded graciously.

Home. A place where everyone she loved resided.

Indeed, that was exactly where she needed to be.

જી

"This is ridiculous, Keir. It is barely a nick. I do not need rest."

From his chair bedside the four-poster bed, Keir stifled a smile at both Maude's impressively dark scowl, and her irritable tone; clearly learned from him as a reluctant patient. Even propped up on pillows in her embroidered nightgown, sporting a linen bandage about her neck and purple salve on her upper arm to help with bruising, she remained the most beautiful woman in Scotland.

More importantly, she was his at long last.

Keir shrugged. "A few hours in bed won't do ye any harm... and remember who made up the story of feeling weak and having a sore neck."

"Bah."

"Callum and Alastair recommended several days at least. Even Isla said an entire day."

She sniffed. "Isla just wanted to steal Sorcha away."

Keir blinked in surprise. "What? I thought the lady was being verra noble."

"Ha. Here's the truth about my beloved daughter-in-law. She was an unexpected child, significantly younger than the other Sutherlands, one who asked endless questions and ignored rules at will. Isla sees Sorcha as the little sister, the eager apprentice she's wanted her whole life. In future, the question will be: can we prise them apart."

"God's blood. The *mayhem*."

"Exactly."

He shuddered. "My hair will be fully silver before year's end. Nae, sooner."

"Black...silver...a combination of the two...I'll still enjoy tangling my fingers in it when you are being wicked," said Maude, her voice husky.

Keir's cock throbbed at the thought—it had surely been a thousand years since their interlude against the chamber door. However, there were things to be said before he fucked her into boneless bliss. Things that he'd waited forever to tell her.

"Aye," he said slowly. "But before any wickedness, I want

to be sure we're in agreement on matters. That ye fully know my mind."

Maude tilted her head, her violet gaze softening. "Very well. Tell me everything so we begin with no misunderstandings."

"I always loathed Donald—"

"Keir! I could count with one hand those who truly liked him...forgive me, I won't interrupt again," she said quickly, when he sent her a look.

"I always loathed Donald," Keir began again. "For he brought home a jewel from England and treated her like a lump o' dirt. Everyone knew of his temper, but most held their tongues. I could not. I urged him to be kind to ye and wee Callum. Usually he ignored me, but I said it so often... one day he demanded to know if I held a torch for the Lady of Glennoe. I should have denied it. But I said naught..."

Maude sucked in an audible breath. Yet she said nothing, just gestured for him to continue.

"That was my downfall," he admitted. "Donald knew my weakness and scratched at it whenever he could. Gave me the worst duties and many night watches in the dead of winter. Thrashed me in front of other guards, so they lost respect for me as captain. I buried my anger in ale and wenches and fistfights, as ye know. But no one was aware Donald had forbidden me ye healing gifts. Battles or training, even illness was more dangerous for me than anyone. Then came that day he threatened to harm ye and I broke his nose. Never will I regret that. But the consequences...the loneliness of banishment, the shame for my family were verra hard. It got so much worse, though, with the raid that stole Burke and Fiona, then the fire that Sorcha lost so many precious keepsakes in...aye, that will long haunt my days. Even after killing Gavin."

"You sacrificed so much more for me than I ever knew,"

whispered Maude, as her fingers traced a restless pattern on the quilt. "Endured so much pain."

Keir shook his head. "I would do so again, over and over, to protect ye. To ensure your happiness. I wanted ye half my life...and now I will love ye until time ends."

A single tear rolled down her cheek. "Oh Keir."

"But I must ask a question in return. Without the opinion of Callum and Alastair involved..." Keir hesitated, the answer so important he could barely get the words out. "Do ye truly wish to wed me? To gather a grizzled old warhorse and an orphaned bairn into your heart with the rest o' ye kin?"

Maude patted the quilt. "Come and sit by me, grizzled warhorse, so I can be certain your old ears hear everything."

So *saucy*.

Keir hauled himself out of the chair and gingerly perched on the side of her intricately carved bed. When the heather mattress and wooden posts didn't protest his bulk, he slid next to her and sank back on the pillows. "Speak, woman."

"Before I answer that particular question, know this," said Maude, as she smoothed a stray lock of hair back from his face. "I scarcely have the words to describe what I feel for you. When we are together...I know I am safe. Protected. But not stifled from being who I am, or ordered to change my manner or obey without question. You honor my gifts rather than being threatened by them. You ask my opinion, and encourage my dreams and desires. Do you know how rare that is? To be with a man who lifts up rather than stomps down?"

Keir tried to speak, but the boulder in his throat was too large, so he just nodded.

"I prayed every day for deliverance from my bad marriage," she continued. "But as you know, it lasted twenty-six long years. When Donald finally died, I prayed every day to feel that miracle that others did, pleasure and comfort in a man's touch. I thought…"

Maude's words trailed off, and she sniffled, dashing a hand across her face.

"Ye thought?" said Keir softly.

"I thought that prayer would never be answered. That I would witness true love only in the trio of Callum, Alastair, and Isla. But then came the morning Sorcha tried to steal from my herb garden and thus began a new path in my life. A path that included the most wondrous pleasure. The most tender comfort. So, if you ask me do I truly wish to wed you, the answer is yes. Because I love you. More than I ever thought possible. High as the heavens and deeper than Loch Etive."

He rubbed his eyes, but the damned things kept watering. "Well. Well then. Aye."

Maude laughed, the sound full of joy. "That was the moment you were supposed to sweep me up in your arms and kiss me until my toes curled, you Highland blockhead. Not say *well, well then, aye*."

Keir cupped her cheek. "I think—"

The bedchamber door burst open, and the laird and Alastair strode in.

"Lady Mother," said Callum, "We wanted to see if you are well, and perhaps make a time to speak with the priest so the banns might be posted—"

"My darling sons," said Maude calmly. "I adore you more than life itself. But if you do not turn on your heel and leave this bedchamber so I can kiss the man I love, I will administer a purging powder so strong that you'll both spend a week in the privy."

The two men gulped and went a shade of green.

"Er…beg pardon, Mother," said Alastair, taking his lover's arm and walking him back toward the door. "As you were."

"We'll knock in future," said the laird, his cheeks flushing a little. "The discussion can wait until tomorrow."

"Yes, it can," said Maude, blowing them a kiss. "Have a wonderful afternoon."

As soon as the door closed and they were alone once more, Keir laughed, unable to suppress his mirth any longer. "Ah, but you're a magnificent woman. Healing the sick and injured, visions from above, outwitting the king, expertly managing a laird and his squire..."

She beamed. "Don't forget holding grizzled warhorses and orphaned bairns close to my heart. Now, where were we. I believe I was about to be kissed until my toes curled?"

Keir brushed his lips chastely across her forehead. "Ye called me a Highland blockhead, angel. I'm not sure I can oblige with toe-curling kisses after such grievous sauciness. In fact...I probably need to consider punishment."

"Grievous sauciness is quite serious. I should get a spanking."

"Indeed. 'Tis only fitting. Then you'll receive my cock hard and deep in that rounded arse of yours."

Maude whimpered, her eyes shining and nipples visibly pressing against the bodice of her nightgown. "And that punishment must happen at once, yes?"

A growl rumbled in his chest. "As ye desire."

CHAPTER 11

Those blunt words. That primitive growl. Keir truly was a wicked Highlander, and she loved it.

Maude moved restlessly in the bed, her night-gown chafing her nipples like sackcloth. This would not do. She had to get rid of it.

Gripping both sides of the bodice, she tore it off then cupped her bare breasts, offering them up to Keir. "Taste me."

He stared at her with such hunger, yet there was more than lust in those hazel eyes. There was love, a heady desire to both possess and worship, and she whimpered again with the need to feel him around her, inside her, no inch untouched.

"Beg pardon?" he asked softly.

Maude pushed the quilt away and went up on her knees. Then she delved a hand between her legs to stroke her rapidly dampening core. "I'm readying myself for your tongue. Ooooh...there'll be honey aplenty."

Keir shook his head. "All I see is an angel misbehaving."

Before she could blink, he'd tumbled her onto her side, then rolled her onto her back. After that, he took a piece of torn nightgown and looped it loosely around her wrists, before placing her hands above her head.

"Oh dear," she said breathlessly, squirming in delight at the playful bondage. "I'm in trouble now."

"Ye certainly are," he replied sternly, placing a hand either side of her head then swooping down for a fierce, open-mouthed kiss.

Her toes curled.

Maude spread her thighs, arching her mound in blatant invitation. But Keir ruthlessly avoided the places she needed him most, first kissing her neck and the thin bandage with aching gentleness then tracing her collarbone with the tip of his tongue. Next, he trailed his mouth along the soft flesh of her upper arms, his beard lightly scratching her skin until she moaned, yearning to receive the same attention to her jewel-hard nipples.

"Keir, please," she said hoarsely.

"Please, what?"

Excitement pulsed through her. Yes, he would make her say the words, to be plain about her desires. Exactly the lover she wanted.

Maude moved sinuously on the quilt, the embroidered fabric abrading her back and heightening her desire. "Pinch my nipples. Hard. Please, my love."

His eyes glittered like gold pieces. "Ye beg so sweetly, angel."

Fortunately, Keir was a benevolent conqueror, his big hands pushing her breasts together as his thumbs rubbed back and forth against the swollen tips. Then at last, pinching them firmly, so wonderfully firmly, she cried out at his skill. It was as though her nipples and the throbbing pearl between her legs were joined by an invisible pleasure rope; every time he pinched, the resulting jolt of sensation arrowed directly to her core and moisture already bathed her most delicate flesh.

But soon she craved more: the rough wet heat of his tongue and lips.

"Suck me," she pleaded, bucking as Keir captured one nipple between his teeth, the raw, grazing motion followed by a soothing lap of his tongue.

As he continued to graze and soothe, her need rose higher and higher. In desperation, Maude tried to free herself from the nightgown restraint so she might bring one hand down to touch herself and gain release. Instead, Keir secured her wrists in an unrelenting grip as he teased the taut, aching peaks, tormenting her further as he stroked her belly, the endless circles moving toward her mound but not quite reaching it. Just when she was ready to threaten *him* with a purging powder, his lips closed around her nipple while his fingertips brushed across her swollen pearl.

Maude gasped at the sudden burst of pleasure; however, she wasn't eased into bliss. No, Keir hurled her into the storm, sucking roughly, abrading her with his beard, all while plunging two fingers in and out of her soaked sheath. Her whole body bowed, her heels dug into the mattress, and she cried out in agonizing relief as a powerful release overcame her.

But her beloved wasn't finished with her.

Sitting back, Keir slowly licked his fingers clean. "Onto your hands and knees, angel. Spread those thighs wide for me."

Maude turned onto her belly and pushed herself up, impatient for his next act. "Hurry," she begged eventually. "Please hurry."

"Shhh," he scolded. "I'm busy admiring this fine arse. But your thighs could be much wider; spread them at once."

She didn't move an inch. "*Make me.*"

"Verra well."

Keir knelt behind her. His palm connected sharply with

her bottom and Maude panted, shocked that the sting enhanced her arousal even further.

"Do that again!" she demanded.

"Wicked woman," Keir muttered, but he granted the boon of several more spanks, each one harder than the last, before cupping her warmed and tingling bottom. "Such a pretty pink. Down on your elbows, now. I want this arse nice and high to fuck."

Maude obeyed his command, shuddering when her tender nipples rubbed against the quilt. But then he parted her bottom cheeks and licked a languid path from swollen pearl to back entrance, his tongue probing inside the tight hole, and her mind whirled away at the sinfully good sensation. "*Keir.*"

As though he had all the time in the world, he lapped at her hole while his fingers circled lazily around her pearl, pushing into her sheath and trailing the copious wetness up to the narrow channel he would soon be entering with his cock. She arched her back, trying to encourage more urgency, but the vexing man merely laughed and gave her two more spanks.

"You'll get my cock when I decide you've earned it," he chided.

Saints alive. She couldn't take much more teasing.

Maude gripped the quilt with both hands, hoping Keir would grant her mercy before she perished of want. So many parts of her body had been coaxed into sharp sensitivity, from her taut nipples to her hot bottom cheeks to her throbbing pearl, that it was nigh-on unbearable. Especially when she couldn't see what he was doing, didn't know which skilled act of licking or stroking, spanking or fingering, she would receive next. "But I *need* it."

"Do ye now?"

"Yes," she moaned, slapping the bed in frustration. "Fuck

me. Fuck my bottom. I want to know what it feels like to be owned there by you."

Keir's indrawn breath was overloud in the bedchamber and she heard laces snap and fabric tearing—another pair of ruined hose. But he didn't penetrate her where he'd promised. Instead, Keir thrust his engorged cock inside her wet sheath with brutal force, before withdrawing just as quickly. He did it again. And again. Tormenting her with a smooth glide but no release.

"Feel how hard I am for ye?" he growled. "So hard it hurts. This sweet cunt makes me ache to fill it with seed, but it's getting my cock all nice and slick before I take your arse."

Maude cried out as pleasure danced on the sizzling edge of pain. Keir's shaft was long and thick at the best of times, but from this angle he felt simply enormous. How would it even fit in her bottom?

When he pressed his cock against her back entrance, she tensed.

"Easy, angel," Keir soothed, stroking her back. "Breathe for me."

Gulping in air, she pushed her bottom against him, whimpering a little when the head eased past the tight ring and forced her shockingly sensitive inner walls to stretch and receive. It burned; oh, how it burned. And yet that bite of pain made her swollen pearl throb harder, made her empty sheath clench in envy. "*More.*"

With a low snarl, Keir gripped her hips and inched deeper and deeper until he was balls-deep inside her bottom. Maude gripped the quilt so tightly her knuckles were white and sweat bathed her skin. She was full. Far too full, yet so achingly close to release.

As though he understood, Keir began to thrust, very, very slowly. In. Out. In. Out.

Maude sobbed in feverish need, begging to be allowed to

spend. He moved one hand between her legs, roughly cupping her mound and caressing her pearl.

It was like she'd been struck by lightning.

Screaming as she reached a peak of pleasure she'd not even dared to dream of, Maude tumbled over the edge and soared to the stars. Keir held her hip, ramming his cock inside her, once, twice, thrice, then with an untamed roar, flooded her bottom with seed.

They both slumped onto the quilt, Keir's bulk flattening her firmly against it. And yet she didn't want to move. Not ever.

"I love you," he rasped, kissing her shoulder. "My angel."

Maude smiled, about all she could do. "And I love you, my wicked Highlander."

❧

When Keir awoke and his stretching arm found nothing but linen sheet, he knew a moment of panic. But as he sat up, his gaze darting about the bedchamber, his heart returned to normal at the sight of Maude kneeling naked at the window, her hands clasped in prayer.

Now, he just stared in reverence.

The afternoon weather wasn't overly warm or bright, yet somehow her body was bathed in a golden glow, her white-blond hair shimmering like a waterfall. As for the smile on her face...well, that would surely put the sun to shame. Had he only thought her the most beautiful woman in Scotland? No one on this earth could compare.

"I can feel your eyes on me, Keir."

"And I can hear a heavenly chorus in the distance."

Maude laughed and tossed her head. "You are most welcome to join me."

"Must I be naked?"

"Well, I enjoy that, but you can wear clothing if you like. On second thought, a pair of ruined hose is an affront to God, so you should probably take them off."

Keir snorted as he stripped off his clothing then ambled over to join her. "I'm sure the Almighty is not so judgmental, unlike his priests."

She shuffled sideways on her velvet cushion so he could kneel beside her. "A truth."

"So," he said slowly. "Are ye praying about anything in particular?"

Maude rested her head on his shoulder. "I'm just...giving thanks. For you and us and Sorcha and my sons and Isla and the grandbabe I'll meet in autumn. Oh yes, and the king."

Keir turned and kissed her forehead. "Aye. A lot to be thankful for...this is a verra nice window. Like having a sun bath. Much better than that dark and gloomy chapel. I'm always afeared that I'll sneeze in a quiet part from the incense."

"Ha. Do not encourage me on dark chapels and dour priests; I might rant for hours. Let us just revel in joy."

After curling an arm about her waist, Keir closed his eyes and succumbed to the warmth streaming through the window. It was just so *peaceful*. Was his healing leg scar tingling? No. Surely not. Just a fanciful thought because he knelt next to a naked angel as she once again murmured words in a language he didn't understand.

Eventually, Maude finished her prayers and squeezed his hand. "We'd best stand up, before our knees creak too loudly."

"Agreed," he said.

They hauled each other to their feet, smiling ruefully at the clicks and creaks, then she walked over to an iron hook next to the bed and returned with a brocade robe. "This will be entirely too small, but might at least cover you until I send for new hose and shirt from the weaving house. Don't put it on yet, though, I'm going to give you a sponge bath."

"That sounds wifely...but we are not yet wed," said Keir cautiously.

Maude led him over to the fireplace. "I do have thoughts on that, but first you must ask me to marry you. Please ask me. It will be the most eager yes ever heard. Shall I speak of my virtues? There are plenty of good reasons to wed a healer."

He stilled. So, this was what bone-deep happiness felt like. Declarations of love and a lusty bedding, sun-drenched prayer windows and the most beautiful woman on earth insisting he wed her. "I'm well aware o' your countless virtues, angel. Not eager to fall to my knee again, though. Have mercy on your grizzled warhorse."

"No need for kneeling, but please do stay warm," said Maude as she hung a bucket of well water over the fireplace to heat, then dashed away to her apothecary, returning with two handfuls of green herbs. "I'd wager this won't even be Scotland's first naked sponge bath betrothal."

Keir sighed in contentment as she bathed him with the warm, fresh-scented water, scrubbing at his shoulders and chest, but gentle, almost teasing around his cock. "That is verra good."

"How is your leg faring?"

"It tingled in front of the prayer window, but other than that, nothing. Not even a twinge when I fought in the clearing. I can hardly believe it, but ye are the best healer in Scotland and an angel, so..."

Maude winked, then kissed his cock. "Not always an angel."

God's blood. He needed to take this woman to wife at once. Even a day without waking up beside her, holding her in his arms, bantering back and forth, would be far too long.

"Ye know," Keir said thoughtfully, "if we didn't want to

fuss about with priests and posting of the banns, there is always an irregular marriage. We write a promise to be together and sign it, have it witnessed by others. However, to be truly legal, I must also bed ye thoroughly."

Maude beamed as she sponged his legs and feet. "Ha! I was going to suggest an irregular marriage. The chapel and its rites hold no sanctity for us, not like my prayer window, so it is perfect. We might have to practice many, many times to ensure the wedding bedding is done properly, though."

"Aye," he said, taking a deep breath before leaning down and clasping her hands in his. "Lady Maude MacIntyre. My beloved. I've waited twenty-six years for this, and now I stand before ye...naked...hoping this will continue to be the best day o' my life. Will ye marry me?"

She sniffled. "Master Keir Wright. I sit before you...also naked...to offer my love and devotion. And to say yes, yes, *yes*, I will marry you."

Swept away in elation, the next few hours passed in a blur. Keir gave her a sponge bath in return, and naturally that turned into a desire to get Maude sweaty and sticky once again, which required a second bath for them both. She sent for more clothing from the weaving house, laughing the entire time at how ridiculous her brocade robe looked on him as it barely covered his arse, and that earned her another spanking. But eventually the fresh garments were delivered, and now he stood dressed in hose, embroidered linen shirt, and a velvet doublet threaded with silver, feeling as grand as the king himself. Maude looked like a queen in a sapphire-blue satin gown with white sleeves, a jewel-encrusted silver girdle, and her hair falling loose down her back.

More importantly, she clutched the parchment scroll they'd written and signed, pledging their lives to one another.

Keir offered his arm. "Let us go and find our family, then. Tell them the news."

He spoke with confidence, but a little sweat trickled down the back of his neck as they strolled to the library. How would Callum react? The laird had seemed quite insistent on them wedding the traditional way with priest and reading of the banns.

"All will be well, Keir," said Maude, patting his hand as they knocked on the library door. "Remember my purging promise."

Laughter rumbled in his chest. "Ye would never."

"They can't be sure of that."

Inside the library, Callum was reading a pile of documents, while Alastair sat nearby polishing Isla's magnificent sword. The Lady of Glennoe herself was lounging in her shirt and hose on a pile of cushions, sharing a dish of sweetmeats with Sorcha.

Keir cleared his throat. "Good afternoon, laird. My lady. Master Alastair. Niece."

They all halted and stared at him with raised eyebrows.

"So very formal, Keir," said Isla merrily. "Something important to declare?"

"Ye look verra grand, Uncle," said Sorcha, sitting up. "And Aunt Maude does, too."

Alastair tilted his head, his gaze narrowing. "Too grand for an afternoon library visit."

"Shhh," said Isla. "Let them speak."

The library became so quiet, they might have heard a butterfly snort.

Keir tugged on his shirt cuff. He wasn't some green lad, why was this so difficult? "Er...I do have something important to declare. Earlier, Maude...that is, the beautiful Lady Maude MacIntyre insisted...nae, consented...er..."

Ach. Everyone just looked bewildered now. He needed to cease the courtly rambling and just be himself. That was who Maude loved, after all.

"Maude and I wed the irregular way," said Keir gruffly. "We have the signed document to be witnessed. We'll all raise a glass of whisky to toast and that's the end of the matter."

Maude giggled. "By the by, we love each other madly and feel truly blessed to have found such happiness at an older age."

He grunted. "Aye. That too."

Callum rose to his feet, his lips twitching. "Well, then. I'd best sharpen the quill. Alastair, pour some whisky. Isla and Sorcha, bring the sweetmeats."

"Ye...don't mind?" said Keir, surprised. "No chapel or banns?"

The laird shrugged. "All I ever wanted was my mother's happiness. You make her happy. There is naught else to consider, really. I know you'll be an excellent grandfather to our babe, too."

Grandfather?

God's blood. Soon there would be bairns everywhere. Wailing. Spewing. Demanding shoulder rides from their grizzled warhorse. Smothering him in hugs.

He swayed a little.

"Quick, give the man a whisky," said Maude, her eyes gleaming in a very non-angelic way.

Keir leaned down, so he might speak directly in her ear. "Such wickedness, wife."

"Forever and ever," she replied serenely. "Husband."

As he captured her lips in a fierce kiss, his new family applauding and cheering around him, Keir allowed himself a smile.

Aye, love was possible for all.

Even wicked Highlanders.

September, 1505

Maude tapped her foot as she adjusted the shoulder strap of her herb satchel for the tenth time, waiting for her husband and niece to join her at the chamber door. "Keir! Sorcha! We're all going to be late!"

Just when she thought she'd have to toss a fishing net and haul them in, they emerged from Sorcha's room.

"I'm here!" said Sorcha, twirling in place. "Do ye like my new tunic?"

"Beautiful. Heather's embroidery really is the best in the clan. But what took you so long, sweetling?"

"I lost my hair ribbon."

"Don't you have several?"

Keir grunted. "She couldnae find the right one. Blue, but not *that* blue."

Maude bit her lip to halt a laugh. It was a discussion had in their niece's chamber several times each week. Keir was becoming much more patient; he only threatened to tie back Sorcha's hair with a dirty old stocking or piece of string every other day now. "Your plait looks lovely."

Sorcha preened. "Everyone wants Uncle Keir to plait their hair now. When he walks me to lessons, they form a line."

Glancing at her husband, Maude raised an eyebrow.

He flushed slightly. "Lads and lasses cannae run about with wild hair while they learn to fight and weave and read. But I must get to training at once. Isla brought wee Lorne yesterday to watch, then lectured me for not being strict enough with footwork. No doubt today, I'll be holding the babe while she makes the guards dance."

As they hurried down the hallway toward the stairs, Maude smiled at the mention of her precious two-week-old grandson. It had been an honor and a joy to help guide him into the world, although Callum and Alastair had refused to wait in the library or even the hallway, insisting on remaining at Isla's side in the birthing chamber. Many, many tears had been shed at the babe's first indignant wail, an heir who would grow up surrounded by love.

"Highly likely," she replied. "You know how Isla is with footwork."

Sorcha pouted. "She told me I stomp like I wear stone boots."

A truth.

"Well, I've heard the calls outside so often, I swear I do them when I walk," said Maude kindly. "At least Lorne is more than content to curl up on his grandfather's shoulder."

"Dinnae ken why it has to be *my* shoulder," Keir grumbled. "The babe's got two fathers."

She snorted. Keir doted on the tiny baby and scowled at anyone—including Callum and Alastair—when they dared to take Lorne away for a walk in the garden or return him to his cradle to sleep. He really was a magnificent grandfather. And uncle. And husband. And lover.

Especially a lover.

Maude's cheeks heated in remembrance of how he'd woken her up that very morning; bringing her to the edge of release over and over with just his tongue, making her suck his cock to a stand, then demanding she ride him to completion. A part of her wondered how each day she wanted him *more* than when they'd first been together in the mountain dwelling, but there was a simple answer to that: each day he made her feel like the most important, the most learned, the most skilled, and the most beautiful woman in the world.

Whether they were discussing healing or sword fighting, ambling about her herb garden gathering plants for a salve or tonic, playing dice or cards with Sorcha, or enjoying a whisky with Callum, Alastair, and Isla in the library, he ensured it was all enjoyable. Even better, they were both starting to feel like a real part of the clan rather than two outsiders. No longer were there whispers of witch or traitor. Those in the village now shared news and recipes, complained about children's antics, and argued over who had the finer bottom: a shepherd or a fisherman. Keir was often invited to hunt, and as a new clan elder alongside his captain duties, helped Callum hear and rule on disputes.

It was...nice. Very nice.

When they reached the castle courtyard, Maude turned to embrace them both. "Keir, I hope you have a good day with our grandbabe...or your sword. Sorcha, I cannot wait to hear what you learn in your lessons. Be good for the scribe."

"Aye, Aunt."

Keir's brow furrowed. "Are ye visiting the broken thumb or the fever, Maude?"

"Both," she laughed.

"Did ye remember something to eat in your satchel? Ye need to eat."

Maude cupped his face and smoothed his beard. The way he cared for her would forever warm her heart. "Yes, I have my little food parcel."

He leaned down and kissed her so soundly that Sorcha groaned and covered her eyes. "*Uncle*! We'll be verra late!"

"Oh, now ye fret about that," said Keir, shaking his head. "I'll see ye soon, angel."

Maude blew them both a kiss and waved, watching them move away to their tasks. Soon she would walk to the village and begin hers, knowing that at the end of the day she would return once more to warmth and laughter with her family and the pleasures of a husband who cared.

Her prayers had been answered.

Love truly was the greatest miracle of all.

ALSO BY NICOLA DAVIDSON

A Rake, His Patron, & Their Muse (#1)

An Earl, His Valet, & Their Wife (#2)

A Lady, Her Lord, & Their Duke (#3)

Regency Standalones

Seven Sinful Nights

Duke for Hire

Her Virgin Duke

Mistletoe Mistress

Joy to the Earl

Once Upon a Promise

Medieval Scotland

Glennoe Highlanders

Wicked Passions (#1)

Her Wicked Highlander (#2)

Scandalous Passions

Tudor novellas

His Forbidden Lady

One Forbidden Knight

Paranormal

Medieval Wolf Kings

Wolf Duke (#1)

Contemporary

Ladies First (erotic short stories)

ABOUT THE AUTHOR

USA Today bestselling author **Nicola Davidson** worked for many years in media and government communications, but hasn't looked back since she decided writing erotic historical romance was infinitely more fun. When not chained to a computer, she can be found ambling along one of New Zealand's beautiful beaches, cheering on the All Blacks rugby team, history geeking on the internet, or daydreaming. If this includes dessert—even better!

Her books have appeared in *USA Today, NPR*, and *Entertainment Weekly*.

Keep up with Nicola's news on Twitter (@NicolaMDavidson) Facebook (Nicola Davidson—Author) Instagram (@NicolaDauthor) or her website www.nicola-davidson.com